THE ONE AND ONLY

The big, flame-haired man drew the Colt with the ivory grip and dropped to one knee.

The man holding the girl down with her arms pinned back offered a poor target. A shot could easily wind up hitting *her*. He lifted the Colt a fraction and aimed at the man's shoulder. Perfect shot! His target flew backward, his shoulder exploding in a shower of blood and bone.

"Goddamn," said the victim's partner, as he yanked at his gun. But the weapon never cleared its holster as a bullet slammed into him.

"It's you, it's got to be," the girl murmured as she was helped to her feet. "Red hair, riding a palomino. There can't be two of you."

"You're right," said the man with the Colt. "Far as I know, I'm the one and only Canyon O'Grady."

CANYON O'GRADY

2

SILVER SLAUGHTER

by

Jon Sharpe

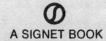

A SIGNET BOOK

NEW AMERICAN LIBRARY

A DIVISION OF PENGUIN BOOKS USA INC.

NAL BOOKS ARE AVAILABLE AT QUANTITY DISCOUNTS WHEN USED TO
PROMOTE PRODUCTS OR SERVICES. FOR INFORMATION PLEASE WRITE
TO PREMIUM MARKETING DIVISION, NEW AMERICAN LIBRARY,
1633 BROADWAY, NEW YORK, NEW YORK 10019.

The first chapter of this book appears in *Cave of Death*, the ninety-
first volume in the *Trailsman* series.

SIGNET TRADEMARK REG. U.S. PAT. OFF. AND FOREIGN COUNTRIES
REGISTERED TRADEMARK—MARCA REGISTRADA
HECHO EN DRESDEN, TN, U.S.A.

SIGNET, SIGNET CLASSIC, MENTOR, ONYX, PLUME,
MERIDIAN and NAL BOOKS are published by
New American Library, a division of
Penguin Books USA Inc., 1633 Broadway,
New York, New York 10019

First Printing, July, 1989

1 2 3 4 5 6 7 8 9

PRINTED IN THE UNITED STATES OF AMERICA

Canyon O'Grady

His was a heritage of blackguards and poets, fighters and lovers, men who could draw a pistol and bed a lass with the same ease.

Freedom was a cry seared into Canyon O'Grady, justice a banner of the heart.

With the great wave of those who fled to America, the new land of hope and heartbreak, solace and savagery, he came to ride the untamed wildness of the Old West.

With a smile or a six-gun, Canyon O'Grady became a name feared by some and welcomed by others but remembered by all . . .

*1859, the Territory of Kansas between the
Missouri border and the Flint Hills,
a land seething with the rage of
the red man and the schemes
of the white . . .*

1

"Now, that's a bit of a strange one," the tall, muscularly built man muttered, his eyes on the road below as he sat astride the pale-bronze horse with the blond mane. A two-seat spring wagon rolled along under his gaze, one man driving, a second man in the rear seat beside a young woman. Nothing unusual there, he had first decided, and then he noticed that the young woman was bound hand and foot. The tall man on the palomino had peered harder and saw she was also gagged with a thick, wide kerchief.

He ran one hand through his thick, flame-red hair, and his lips pursed as his snapping blue eyes continued to peer down at the wagon below. "I'd say we ought to have a closer look at that, Cormac, lad," he murmured, and edged the palomino down the slope. When he was halfway down, he realized the wagon was moving much faster than it had seemed from above; he spurred the pale-bronze horse into a trot, cut across the slope, and headed downward again to reach the road just as the wagon rounded a curve. The driver reined to a halt as the big man on the palomino blocked his way.

"Afternoon, gents," the big, redheaded man said affably. "The name's Canyon O'Grady." He took in the two men with one quick, practiced glance. The man holding the reins was a broad figure with a thrusting jaw, the second man thinner of face and build with a three-day stubble and a long, hooked nose. Both men wore wariness on their faces at once. "I saw you from the slope," Canyon O'Grady said, and his eyes went to the young woman. "I'm a curious man." He smiled.

"Be curious someplace else," the one holding the reins growled.

Canyon O'Grady's patient smile stayed. "That'd be hard to do, seeing as you're all here and I'm here," he said.

The girl wore a brown dress with a square neck, he saw, and she had a somewhat thin body under the dress but high, rounded breasts and nicely turned calves. Light-brown hair, brown eyes, and a short nose was all he could see of her face behind the wide kerchief that served as a gag.

"As I said, I'm a curious man, and right now I'm curious why you have this lass trussed up like a pig at a barbecue," he said, his voice still mild.

"It's none of your damn business," the one with the thrusting jaw said.

"Now, hold on, Fenton. You can't blame the man for being curious," the hook-nosed one cut in, plainly eager to avoid the possibility of trouble. "She's wanted for murder back in Nobs Corner," he said to Canyon. "Fact is, she's a desperate, rotten woman. Killed a man in cold blood, she did."

"And we're bringing her back," Fenton chimed in quickly. "She took off after she'd done her killin'."

Canyon looked at the young woman, who was making unintelligble sounds under the gag. She shook her head violently from side to side as her eyes plainly pleaded with him for help. "Why the gag?" Canyon asked mildly.

"Because all she does is curse and scream. She's

got a rotten mouth. We just had to gag her,'' the hook-nosed man said.

Canyon's eyes returned to the young woman again, fixing on the brown eyes that stayed round with pleading. She continued to make muffled sounds of protest under the kerchief. "You lads deputies?" he asked, bringing his gaze back to the two men.

"That's right," Fenton snapped. Then, catching the big red-haired man's gaze, he added, "We don't bother with badges in Nobs Corner."

"I see," Canyon said, and saw the man beside the girl catch hold of her as she twisted and tried to fall from the wagon seat. "Well, I'm not one to interfere with deputies carrying out the law." He smiled and heard the stifled shouts from behind the gag. "Good day to you, gents," he said pleasantly, and ignored the girl as she twisted and writhed with frantic desperation. He turned the palomino, crossed the road, and disappeared into the trees on the other side. When he was deep enough in the woods, he halted and peered back to watch the wagon roll on again, the driver snapping the reins hard over the horse.

O'Grady ran one hand along the warm, powerful neck of the pale-bronze horse. "I've a bad odor in my nose," he murmured. "Let's follow along a spell, lad." Staying in the trees, he began to follow the wagon, which stayed on the road for another half-mile or so and then abruptly turned off onto a steep hillside.

Canyon stayed back in the trees as he climbed after the wagon and watched it struggle up the steepness. He moved to the right as he followed and spurred the palomino on a little faster as the wagon reached a high ledge of relatively flat land. The man at the reins drove the wagon hard along the ledge, then suddenly made a half-circle and turned the horse to face the edge of the ledge, where he reined to a halt.

Canyon spurred the palomino higher up on the hill and halted where he could look down on the wagon and the ledge. A furrow dug into his brow.

The wagon had halted with the horse facing a sheer drop of hundreds of feet into a rock-filled gorge below. As Canyon watched, still frowning, the two men climbed from the wagon and the driver, Fenton, began to unhitch the horse. When he finished, he drew the horse to one side and returned to the wagon where the hook-nosed man had already started to put his shoulder to the rear wheel.

Canyon instantly spurred the palomino forward as one hand went to the holster at his side. But he halted still out of view as Fenton paused and stepped back.

"Wait, we've got to untie her. Can't have her found all tied up," he said. He climbed into the wagon, and drawing a skinning knife from his pocket, he cut the young woman's bonds. She erupted and tried to leap from the wagon but the hook-nosed one caught hold of her, punched her in the stomach, and she fell back with a gasp of pain. Canyon saw the kerchief come loose to reveal full lips and a nice chin, albeit her face was a shade thin.

"Bastards," she flung out at the two men. She tried to leap from the wagon again, but Fenton caught her, knocking her back in with a sharp slap.

"Wait. Let's enjoy her first," the hook-nosed one said. "Shit, there's nothin' to lose by it."

Fenton paused, his eyes on the young woman. "Why not?" he said, and as a grin spread across his face, he reached up and yanked the girl from the wagon. The hook-nosed one pinned her arms behind her on the ground and Fenton tried to pull her dress up. She managed to twist and Fenton took a kick on the side of his leg.

"Hold her, dammit," Fenton barked as the girl continued to twist and kick out. He caught one of her legs in his hands, twisted it, and she cried out in pain as he managed to push her dress up.

Canyon got a glimpse of nice calves and round knees as she continued to kick and writhe.

"Enjoy it, bitch. It's gonna be your last lay," Fenton snarled, yanking the front of his Levis open. He lowered himself to his knees over the still-struggling figure of the girl, pushed her legs open with his body, and clawed at her underclothes.

"Time to interrupt the party, one-sided as it is," Canyon muttered, and spurred the palomino closer. Both men were too intent on their pleasures to hear him, and as he neared the ledge, he swung from the horse, landed silently on the balls of his feet, and ran forward. He drew the big Colt with the ivory grips and swore under his breath as he halted, dropping to one knee.

Fenton, clumsily writhing with the girl, offered a poor target. A shot could easily wind up also hitting the young woman. Canyon lifted the Colt a fraction and took aim at the man who held her arms pinned back. He fired and the man screamed in pain as he flew backward, his left shoulder exploding in a shower of blood and bone.

"Goddamn," Fenton said in surprise as he looked up and whirled from straddling the girl. He half-rose, still hanging out of his pants, and yanked at his gun. The weapon never cleared its holster. O'Grady's shot slammed into his midsection and he doubled in two as he flew backward.

Canyon had dropped to the ground the moment he fired, and heard the shot from the right whistle over his head. The hook-nosed man, his left shoulder a gaping red hole, lay on one elbow, but he had managed to yank his gun free and he fired again from his near-prone position.

Canyon dived to one side as another shot whistled nearby and came up firing a burst of shots. The man quivered, his body bucking, and then he lay still.

Canyon rose to his feet and was beside the young woman in one long stride. He reached his hand out and pulled her to her feet. Her eyes, still wide with fear, blinked as she peered hard at him. "It's you, it's got to be," she murmured. "Red hair, riding a palomino. There can't be two of you."

"You're right. So far as I know, I'm the one and only Canyon O'Grady," the big, flame-haired man said.

"You're the one they're after," she said.

Canyon frowned back. "It did seem to me that you were the one they were going to throw over the cliff," he said.

"Yes, but that was only because they knew I knew about you," she returned.

"Whoa, now. Maybe you'd best be starting at the beginning," he said, and kept his voice mildly curious while the young woman's words set off an alarm inside him. "Let's try starting with your name," he said, and smiled.

"Amy Dillard. I work in the saloon at Nobs Corner," she said. "That's where I heard about you."

"Heard what about me?" Canyon asked.

"That they were going to ambush you at Three Oaks Bend," Amy Dillard said.

Canyon kept his face expressionless, but it took an effort. Three Oaks Bend was exactly where he was headed, a trail marker in the instructions that had been given him. "Fill it in more, lass. Put some flesh on the bones of it," he said.

Amy Dillard took a moment to brush her hair back

and straighten her dress. He had been right about nice rounded breasts, he took note. "I wait tables at the saloon," she said, paused, and peered at him. "Just that," she added defensively. "That's one of my problems there. I don't do what they'd like me to do. I'm particular who I do things with. It's a grubby, sleazy little place and I hate it."

Canyon nodded sympathetically. Amy Dillard was the kind who'd take her own way to things.

"Anyway, these men, six or seven of them, were at one of the tables having a very serious conversation. I was behind the door to the storeroom and I heard them talking about how they were going to ambush and kill somebody at Three Oaks Bend. One was giving the plan to the others and he described you and your horse."

"He never mentioned my name?" Canyon inquired.

"Never. I got the feeling that all he had was a description," Amy said. "Anyway, one of them suddenly noticed me, and they stopped talking. I had to pass them on my way from the storeroom and they stopped me. They asked if I'd heard anything they were talking about."

"You said no, of course," Canyon put in.

"That's right." Amy nodded. "But I wondered then if they believed me. I wasn't sure, of course, so this morning, after I got dressed, I decided to take the spring wagon that belongs to the saloon and set out to try to find you. But they were watching me and those two set on me a few miles back. You know the rest."

"Not all of it. A few things don't answer right," Canyon said, and she waited. "Why didn't they just take a six-gun to you? Why all the bother about tossing you off the cliff in a wagon?"

"A lot of people know me in Nobs Corner. If I were found shot dead, there'd be posses out and a lot of questions. They plainly didn't want that. An accident, a runaway horse and wagon, means no posses, nobody chasing after anyone,'' Amy Dillard said. ''But it didn't work, thanks to you.''

''I'd say Lady Luck deserves the credit. She had me at the right place at the right time,'' Canyon said.

''But you did the rest,'' she said.

He shrugged and his snapping blue eyes peered at her. ''One more question, lass,'' he said. ''Why'd you come running to warn me? Damn few pretty young ladies are so full of good deeds.''

''It wasn't just that,'' Amy said, an air of reluctant confession coming into her voice. ''I told you I wanted to get away from Nobs Corner, far away. I need money to do that, enough for a long stage ticket. I figured that if I found you and warned you about the ambush you'd reward me in good hard cash.''

''You're honest, I'll give you that,'' Canyon said.

''Hell, saving your life ought to be worth a reward.'' She frowned.

''It is, and I'm grateful to you for what you tried to do. But it seems to me that I'm the one that did the saving.''

Amy Dillard frowned at him for a long moment. ''I suppose that's true enough,'' she murmured. ''You saying I didn't really do anything?''

''You tried. I did more than that,'' Canyon said mildly. ''Intentions are one thing, deeds are another.'' He watched her turn his words inside her, pretty face wreathed in a deep frown.

''All right, but trying's worth something.''

He smiled at the doggedness in her. ''It is,'' he agreed.

''The way they talked about dry-gulching you, I thought you were probably somebody rich,'' Amy muttered.

"Proof that logic can lead one to wrong answers." Canyon laughed and Amy made an unhappy face.

"Why were they out to dry-gulch you, then?" she asked.

"I'm expected someplace. It seems somebody didn't want me to get there."

"Where's that?"

"That's not for talking about," Canyon said, and Amy shrugged.

"Look, I'll settle for your taking me as far as you can. That's not asking too much," she said.

"Ordinarily, no, but I can't, Amy. I've someplace to be, and it's important. I can't spend time squiring young ladies around. I've time to make up," Canyon said. "I'm sorry, I really am. And I still have the problem of Three Oaks Bend. I have to go there to find my way from it."

"There'll still be four or five of them waiting," Amy said. "I could help you, somehow, someway."

He smiled at her. "Still trying for that reward?"

"Why not? Maybe helping is worth more than trying." She shrugged and a half-pout touched her lips.

Canyon thought for a moment. "Maybe you could help . . ." He saw the excitement flood into Amy Dillard's face.

"I know I could," she said, and he let one hand push a straying brown lock of hair back from her face. She had a combination of womanly determination and little-girl eagerness that gave her an appealing quality.

"Thanks again for the trying," he said.

"Thanks for the saving," she returned, and reached up, pressed her lips on his in a quick kiss of soft wetness, and then stepped back.

"There are all kinds of rewards." Canyon smiled.

"There are," she said. "Now I've got to go back and get my things and bring the wagon back."

He let a deep sigh escape him. "I'm already thinking I've made a mistake," he grumbled as he strode to the horse and hitched the animal back to the wagon. He climbed onto the front seat, Amy beside him, and took the reins. The powerful pale-bronze palomino trailed along behind the wagon. Canyon drove down from the ridge and on the land below, Amy pointed south.

"About five miles," she said, and cast a sideways glance at the man beside her, letting her eyes linger on a face with the touch of a rogue in its handsomeness, a wide mouth quick to smile, and a voice that held a lilt to remember. But she had seen the snapping blue eyes turn ice-floe cold and his ivory-gripped Colt spit death with the speed and accuracy of a rattler's strike. Maybe he wasn't the rich merchant she had expected, but he was no ordinary man, Amy Dillard pondered. Even his name was unusual, made of echoes and questions.

"Tell me about Canyon O'Grady," she said. "You can start with that name. Where'd you get it?"

"My mother gave it to me before she and Pa left Ireland to come here. She wanted a name that would sound like the new, great land she'd admired for so long," the big man said. "Father Rearden baptized me Michael Patrick, but she'd have none of that."

"Your folks run from the potato famine in Ireland?"

"And from the British. Pa was a leader in the Young Ireland Movement, a personal friend of Padraic Pearse and Thomas Davis, the bard of Sinn Fein," Canyon said. "When he came here, he went to work back East building the railroads. But that wasn't for me. When the time came, I rode west, out into the untamed places. I've always had a love of new places, things I've never seen."

"You came out just to roam around?" Amy questioned.

"Let's say I'm a tinker." Canyon laughed.

Her probing frown stayed. "A tinker? Traveling about mending pots and pans? I'm not believing that at all. I don't see any bag of tools on you."

"A mere detail," he said airily.

"Since when do people set up ambushes to kill tinkers?" Amy pressed, and Canyon laughed inwardly. She was quick and sharp.

"Let's say I'm a tinker of souls, a mender of wrongs. And that can sometimes cause problems."

"Is that all the answer you're giving me?"

"There is no more."

"Hell there isn't," she muttered, and broke off the subject as the town came into view. It was a grubby little place, Canyon saw, a carbon copy of a thousand others that seemed to spring up wherever men's trails crossed often enough.

Amy directed him to the saloon. As he pulled up outside, a man strode from the building. Grayish hair with a red, bloated face and a sizable paunch, he fastened a furious glare at Amy.

"Conkers. He owns the place," she muttered to Canyon.

"What's the idea of taking the wagon without asking me, girl?" the man thundered.

"I couldn't ask you. That big oaf of yours wouldn't let me in to ask," Amy tossed back.

"Watch your damn tongue, you little bitch," Conkers roared and Canyon saw another man emerge from the saloon, a large square shape with a heavy face and the kind of eyelids that seemed perpetually half-lowered. Thick lips hung partly open, and Canyon thought of the term Amy had used. It seemed appropriate enough.

"Here's your wagon back, safe and sound," Amy said to Conkers. "I'm quitting."

"Hell you are, girl. Nobody quits unless I let them," Conkers snapped.

"You can't do that," Amy said, but Canyon caught the edge of uncertainty in her voice.

"That's the way it is. That's the way it's always been at my place," the man said.

Amy turned to Canyon. "Can he do that?" she asked.

"You sign a contract of any kind?" Canyon asked her.

"No." She frowned as if the mere thought were ridiculous.

"Then you can go anytime you like," Canyon told her.

"Who the hell are you to butt in, mister?" Conkers interrupted. "You mind your own goddamn business."

"I'm doing that, sort of," Canyon said mildly.

"Get the hell out of my wagon," the man barked.

"Of course," Canyon said amiably, and swung to the ground as Conkers turned to the big oafish figure.

"Teach him about minding his own business, Zeb," Conkers ordered.

The man started toward Canyon at once, his thick lips parting in something between a grin and a grimace. He moved forward with heavy arms dangling loosely.

"He looks a lot bigger from down here," Canyon remarked.

Conkers grinned with anticipation.

Canyon braced himself, powerful shoulder muscles tensing. His short, right uppercut shot out to land flush on the thick-jawed face, and Zeb went down. "He looks a lot stupider, too," Canyon added with a glance at Conkers.

He turned to Amy. "Go get your things," he said, and she hopped from the wagon and started toward the saloon. But the oafish-faced figure pushed to his feet. Canyon took a step back as the man plodded toward him, this time with arms upraised. O'Grady admitted to some surprise, inwardly. His blow would have kept most men down, and he easily avoided a long, clumsy right swing.

"Break him in half, Zeb," Conkers called out.

The thick-armed oaf swung again, a left and a right, and Canyon parried both blows, ducked backward, and Zeb rushed, throwing a hard left hook. Canyon's left that crossed over it was a lightning-fast, snapping left. It landed high on the man's cheekbone, and a streak of red instantly began to slide down his heavy jaw. He halted, blinked, and Canyon's right smashed into his nose. The man staggered backward, the front of his face suddenly scarlet, and Canyon glimpsed the space between the upraised arms. He drove a whistling, straight right forward that landed on the point of Zeb's heavy jaw. The oafish figure staggered again, stiffened, and fell as a tree falls, sending up a cloud of dust as he hit the ground. This time he remained unmoving and Canyon half-turned to where Amy stared wide-eyed.

"I thought you were getting your things," he said. She spun and ran into the saloon. Canyon's eyes went to Conkers and he gestured to the prone figure. "You shouldn't encourage him to take on more than he can handle. You'll ruin his self-confidence," Canyon said mildly.

"I'll remember this, mister," Conkers growled, but Canyon heard the hollowness behind the threat.

"I hope you will," he said pleasantly as Amy came

from the saloon with a canvas sack slung over one shoulder. He took it from her, and tied it to Cormac's saddle horn, and followed her onto the palomino.

The oafish figure was beginning to stir as Canyon rode away, aware of the warm softness of Amy Dillard as she leaned back against him. He put the palomino into a gentle trot and felt her relax against him, the tension going out of her body. The sun became a soothing warmth as they rode and he cut across a long stretch of prairie.

"How long to Three Oaks Bend?" she asked.

"We might make it by late afternoon. We have to make a stop in Hoskinville. You're going to need a horse," Canyon said.

"I don't mind riding like this."

"You'll need a horse for what I want you to do."

She accepted the answer and half-turned to look up at him. "Thanks for standing up for me back there," she said.

"Seemed only right," Canyon said.

"You always do what's right?"

"That depends." He laughed. "I try to combine them."

"Combine what?"

"Principles and pleasure," Canyon said. "Some folks think they don't go together. I think they ought to."

She turned another long glance at him. "I'm thinking you could make them go together. I'd like to know more about you, Canyon O'Grady," she said. "More than those charming stories you've told me."

"Knowing less is better, sometimes." He smiled.

"Not to me," Amy said, settling back against him again. She rode in comfortable silence and he enjoyed the touch of her round little rear against his crotch as he shared the saddle with her.

They reached Hoskinville later in the day, a small town that was not much more than a glorified trading post and didn't even sport a saloon. But there were two wranglers there who kept their own remudas alongside the town with horses for sale, and Canyon halted before the first one.

A man with a length of straw in his mouth moved toward them from inside the stockade, where a collection of horses tried to stay quiet in the heat of the sun. Canyon glanced across the herd. They went from ordinary to less-than-ordinary, he saw, but he wasn't in the market for anything of quality. "Something cheap that can still take a day's riding," he said, and the man pointed to a dark-brown gelding. Canyon noticed the swellings just above the fetlocks on both forelegs and shook his head. An old dapple-gray drew the man's next gesture, but Canyon heard the horse wheeze as it moved. He gave the man a chiding glance.

"All right." The wrangler shrugged and caught hold of a brown mare. Canyon swung to the ground and scanned the horse with a practiced eye. He saw a good, sound animal, sturdy-legged, with a good spring of rib, a horse much better than the others in the herd. "Ten dollars," the man said, and saw Canyon's moment of surprise. "You said cheap," he muttered.

"So I did. Sold," Canyon said. The wrangler added the purchase of a worn saddle and finally turned the horse over to Amy. She climbed onto the horse and Canyon watched the mare move nicely for her. He paid the wrangler his fee and returned to the palomino.

"Southwest," he said to Amy and she came up to ride alongside him. He kept a nice, steady pace and enjoyed watching her nicely rounded breasts move in unison as she rode.

"What is it you'll want me to do?" she asked.

"Nothing that won't come natural to you." Canyon smiled.

"What's that mean?" she half-pouted.

"We'll talk more about it later," he said, and quickened their pace.

The sun had begun to slip over the low hills when Canyon moved into the hill country at the edge of the flatlands. He continued on for another half-hour in the low hills, then he slowed, peered down and forward, and picked out the three big oak trees. Still staying in the low hills, he moved closer and saw the three oaks grew in a cluster with three roads that came together at the base of the trees, each turning to go on in their own direction. He was to take the one that turned a sharp right, but his eyes moved on to the thin line of hawthorns not more than ten yards from the three oaks.

"I don't see anybody," Amy half-whispered.

"They're there," Canyon said.

"You see them?"

"No. They're in that line of hawthorns."

"How do you know? I don't see anything," Amy said.

"You don't have to see a rattler in a woodpile to know he's there," Canyon said. "That's the only place for them to spring an ambush here." He swept the low hills again and moved forward as Amy spurred her horse after him. He halted a dozen yards on but still inside the trees on the low hill. "I'm going to stay right here," he said to Amy. "You go back down to the three oaks and ride into the open."

"They'll see me," Amy protested.

"That's right. I'm betting the minute they see you they'll figure something went wrong and they'll come charging out after you."

"Then what?"

"You see that deer trail there?" Canyon asked, and

pointed to the narrow path six yards away. Amy nodded and he peered on through the trees. "I took note that it goes all the way down to the flatland. You run when they come after you, take that deer trail, and lead them right up here. I'll do the rest." Amy nodded again and he patted her shoulder. "Go down, ride into the open, and then hightail up the deer trail," he repeated.

"I'm to be the lure, enticing them to chase me," Amy said, her eyes narrowed at him. "That's what you meant by it'll be natural to me."

"Enticing is natural to all women," Canyon said. "This is just a variation. Now get moving."

She tossed him a glance of disagreement and turned the mare around and started back down the hill. Canyon moved his horse closer to the edge of the trees on the other side of the deer trail, where he could see her making her way down the hillside. He lost her when she reached the bottom, and brought his gaze back to the three oaks. He was concentrating on them when Amy came into view again, riding slowly, crossing directly in front of the row of hawthorns. It took a few moments and Amy had ridden past the oaks, but it happened: the horsemen burst from the low hawthorns. Four of them, Canyon counted. They raced after Amy and Canyon saw her put the mare into a gallop. The horse moved with good speed and Canyon waited till he saw her reach the bottom of the deer trail and start up the narrow pathway.

The four pursuers raced onto the trail after Amy and had to fall into single file because of the narrowness of the passage. Canyon moved the palomino back across the deer trail to the other side, unholstered the big Colt with the ivory grips, and waited. Amy came into sight first, riding hard up the trail, but the four pursuers had closed ground. Canyon raised the pistol.

The dry-gulchers had been waiting to gun him down without a moment's hesitation and he had no qualms about paying them back in kind.

Amy raced past in front of him, then the first two of her pursuers. Canyon fired, two shots, and both men flew from their horses almost in unison. The third man came into sight. He was trying to yank his horse to a halt, but Canyon's shot struck him full in the chest as he turned to the trees. He toppled back over the horse's rump in a shower of red. The fourth dry-gulcher had been back farther than the others, and Canyon moved forward to see the man had managed to come to a stop and wheel his horse around.

The man started to race down the trail, a long green kerchief around his neck blowing back, and Canyon started to send the palomino after him when Amy's scream split the air. He turned in the saddle to see the mare racing in uncontrollable panic as Amy clung desperately to the reins. O'Grady flung a glance at the man racing away. He could still be caught, Canyon knew, but Amy's scream exploded his thought and he wheeled the palomino in a tight circle. He sent the horse into a gallop after the panicked mare as Amy clung to a precarious grip.

If the horse threw her, she'd have broken bones and maybe a smashed face. If she were smashed against a tree, she could be killed. Either way, she was only fingertips away from disaster, and he kept the palomino racing forward. Though the terrified mare ran with far more than her normal speed, the big, bronze-skinned horse closed the distance quickly and Canyon's lips pulled back in a grimace. There was almost no space on the trail to come alongside the mare. Canyon let the palomino come up to the mare's racing hindquarters and saw Amy almost lose her grip on the reins as the horse swerved.

Canyon inched forward as close as he dared without running the palomino into the mare's flying hooves; he gathered himself and half-rose in the saddle. With a shout, he leapt forward, cleared the palomino's neck, and landed on the mare's rump. He got one arm around Amy's waist before he dived sideways from the mare, yanking the young woman with him. He hit the ground on his side, one arm still around Amy, and he heard her gasp of pain as she came down with him. But he had avoided the trunk of a hackberry only inches from where he'd landed, and he pushed onto one knee and pulled Amy with him. Her arms circled his neck and she clung to him, her slender body trembling.

"Oh, God," she breathed. "I couldn't get control of her."

Canyon grunted wryly. "Now I know why I got that sound a mare so cheap," he said. "She's gun-shy." He got to his feet and pulled Amy with him as the palomino trotted over to him. "Seems that we're back to one horse," Canyon said, and helped Amy into the saddle. "Let's get out of here," he said, and climbed into the saddle behind her.

Dusk was settling fast over the hills. He rode down to the flatland, held a fast canter, and as night began to blanket the terrain, he found a spot to make camp in a clump of slippery elm near a brook. He had some dried beef jerky in his saddlebag and shared it with Amy. When she finished eating, she leaned back on her elbows under the moonlight and regarded him with a long, probing expression.

"What happens now?" she asked.

"You wanted money to get away from these parts. I'll be giving it to you. You've earned it."

"You'd have gotten the last one if it hadn't been for me."

"If it hadn't been for that damn mare," Canyon corrected her.

"I guess you'll never find out who hired those dry-gulchers," Amy said.

"I'll find out, somewhere down the line."

"I could stay on helping you."

"I'm afraid not, lass. I'm expected alone, and I'll work better staying that way," Canyon said.

Amy's eyes stayed on him. "I've never met anyone like you, Canyon O'Grady, and I never will again, I'm sure."

"Then you ought to make the most of it," Canyon said, and his snapping blue eyes held a twinkle.

"I agree," Amy said, and sat up. "It's a hot night."

"It is," Canyon agreed. "And that's a non sequitur if I ever heard one."

"What's a non sequitur?" Amy questioned.

"A Latin phrase that means what was said doesn't connect with what was said before it," Canyon explained.

"What I said connects," Amy returned, and he felt the tiny furrow begin to slide across his forehead as he saw her fingers begin to undo the top button of her dress. She went down to the next, then the next, and quickly had the top of her dress opened. She half-shrugged her shoulders, shimmied, and the top of the dress came off, to tumble down to her waist.

Canyon smiled as he took in the sight of her, breasts not overly large but high and nicely rounded, each tipped with a light-pink nipple on a matching pink circle. He saw shoulders a little bony, a rib cage with the ribs plainly showing, and as she suddenly rose and slid the rest of the dress and her underclothes off, a body that skirted the edge of being skinny. A flat abdomen led down to a surprisingly thick black triangle that looked almost misplaced on her leanness, legs that avoided being sticklike with the vibrancy of youth and smooth white flesh, and a round little rear that seemed to embrace all the fullness the rest of her lacked.

But, naked, she brought her own brand of attractiveness. She fell to her knees beside him with brightness in her brown eyes. "Does it connect now, Canyon?" she asked.

"It does." He laughed and closed his hands around the thin shoulders. He drew her to him and her lips were opened, waiting and willing, as he pressed his mouth to her. He felt her hand opening the buttons of his shirt and he helped her undo the gun belt, open trousers, and shed his clothes while her lips stayed against his, her tongue quickly sliding forward, touching, darting back, touching again, caressing his lips, urgent messenger of wanting. Naked, he felt her body come against his and heard her gasp of delight at the touch of skin to skin, and she pressed harder into him, the high, full breasts flattening under the pressure, tiny pink nipples warm points against his chest.

He put a hand behind her back and brought her around, pressed her gently on the soft grass, and felt the warm night air blow over him. His mouth left hers and began to wander down her slender neck, across the prominent contours of her breastbone, and down to one round, high breast. He touched lips to the pink point already standing up in welcome, and Amy cried out, a tiny, high-pitched sound of delight and anticipation.

Canyon let his lips open and his tongue press down on the pink tip, circle its smoothness. "Oh, oh, God . . . oh, oh yes . . . mmmmmm," Amy cried out, her voice high and suddenly growing louder as he pulled the rest of the round, smooth mound into his mouth. Little half-screams came from her as he caressed with lips and tongue and his hand moved slowly down the center of the flat body, circled the tiny indentation in the flat belly, and moved down to push through the thick, fibrous bush. "Aaaaah, ah, aaaaah," Amy cried out, the high cries suddenly dropping in pitch.

His hand touched one lean thigh and her legs moved at once, opening, falling apart, and he felt her hips thrust upward. "Touch me . . . take me, oh, God," Amy half-groaned, half-cried, and when his hand cupped the dark, moist warmth of her, she screamed in the delight of touch and the joy of anticipation. He moved deeper, along the lubricious lips, and Amy's fingers dug into his back. Her thin legs came together, fell apart again, and he felt himself hard against the smoothness of her thighs when she suddenly twisted, a deep cry wrenched from her throat, and she was atop him, plunging herself onto him with an almost wild frenzy, sinking all of her over his throbbing shaft.

"Oh, God, oh, God," Amy said in a kind of screamed chant, repeating the words over and over in between gasps of pleasure. She pumped and thrust, her round rear slamming down onto his thighs each time, and her brown hair fell forward, half-obscuring her face so that her cries seemed to be coming from a diffused, abstract being. But there was nothing abstract about her touch, her enveloping, exciting torrent of flesh as she bucked harder and harder, the high, round breasts shaking.

"Come with me, Canyon," he heard her cry. "Now, now, oh, God, now." He felt her thin thighs clasp hard against him and her lean body stretched upward as she thrust her head back. Her contractions of ecstasy enveloped him and his hands reached up to grasp her high, round breasts. "Aaaaiiiii . . ." Amy screamed, and he let himself surge with her, entered the moment with her, time and flesh suddenly vanishing and only sensation remaining, consuming the world with its

30

transient volatility. Her pumping halted, her body tingling, and finally, with a deep cry, she fell forward over him, breasts against his face, and lay there panting, gulping in the aftermath of ecstasy. "Oh, God," Amy groaned as she finally fell to his side, her breath still a gasping sound. "Damn, that was good," she murmured.

"It was indeed," Canyon agreed, and gently caressed her breasts as he lay raised on one elbow. Her almost skinny body in the moonlight seemed hardly thin at all now, but made of lean loveliness and fashioned of tensile strength.

"Did I make the most of it, Canyon O'Grady?" Amy smiled.

"You certainly did, lass," he said, and she curled her leg around him.

"Where did you learn about words such as non sequitur?"

"My father made two long visits back to Ireland. He took me with him and deposited me with the Benedictine friars to be educated. They taught me that knowledge is a blessing but knowledge without wisdom is a burden," Canyon said.

"Take me with you. I know I can help," Amy said.

"You're all kinds of temptress, Amy Dillard." Canyon laughed. "But it's for me to go alone, as I told you before."

She returned a half-pout. "Is that knowledge or wisdom?"

"Some of both," he said, and cupped one high, round breast in his hand.

She responded at once, a soft gasp, and then her lips found his, her body growing electric instantly. He made love to her again, slowly, prolonging every impermanent moment until Amy Dillard screamed once more in complete and utter satisfaction to finally lay beside him in the languorous warmth of the body drained, the senses emptied.

"Maybe you are a tinker, Canyon O'Grady," she murmured into his chest. "But I say you're a tinker of hearts, mending all the ones you break."

"I'll take that as a compliment." Canyon chuckled and gathered her against him. "Now get some sleep, lass."

"That won't be hard," she murmured, and proved her words by falling into a deep sleep in moments.

Canyon lay awake only a little longer. He wanted to go over what had brought him to the Kansas Territory, let his mind turn over thoughts, but he decided that could wait till the morning. Such complex thoughts would only be an intrusion on the quiet glow of the moment, and he let himself join Amy in the sleep of the satisfied.

2

Amy woke with him as the warm rays of the morning sun filtered through the trees. Canyon enjoyed watching as she washed in the stream, and when she stretched out on the grass to let the sun dry her, the invitation was plain in her eyes and in her every movement. But he let the cold water of the stream help him push away the temptation. He had been delayed too long now. It was time to go on.

When he finished washing, he used a towel from his saddlebag and Amy pulled clothes over her sun-dried body with reluctant acceptance.

"We'll pass through Bartlestown. There's a stage from there that'll take you all the way into Colorado if you've such a mind," Canyon told her. He drew a roll of bills from a small sack in his saddlebag and handed them to her.

She took the money, counted it, and clung to him for a long moment. "It's real generous, Canyon."

"Use it carefully. Find a patch of happiness with it, Amy," he said, and climbed onto the palomino with her. He headed west, turned south for a while, and came to Bartlestown by noon as Amy rode in silence with him. He reined up before the stage depot, and a heavy-waisted man called out an answer to his question before he asked it.

"Stage for the border's due in an hour," the man said.

"You do much mind-reading?" Canyon laughed.

"All the time. Folks pull up here for only one reason," the stagemaster returned blandly.

"The young lady will want a ticket for one," Canyon said, and swung Amy to the ground.

"Here you are, miss," the stagemaster said as he punched a hole in a small piece of cardboard and handed it to Amy.

"I'm going on. Time's important now," Canyon told her, and she nodded understanding, her chin thrust up firmly. He leaned down from the saddle and she clung to him until he gently pulled free. "I won't forget your trying to help," he said.

"I won't be doing much forgetting, either, Canyon O'Grady," Amy said, and she waved at him as he rode away. She quickly became a small, thin figure staring after him as he kept the palomino at a fast trot.

He smiled to himself as he rode out across the flatland. Amy Dillard would make out in the world. She had a quick, self-serving, opportunistic mind, but a good heart to go with it. She'd never go too far down the wrong path.

He turned off thoughts of Amy and let his blue eyes sweep the land as he held a steady pace.

The Kansa Indians once held this land, and the white man had named it after them. But they had never been great warriors and were reduced to a few tribes these days. The Pawnee ruled this land now. The Kiowa and the Osage stayed pretty much in west Kansas and the Shoshone could turn up anyplace. But this was mainly Pawnee territory, and the Pawnee, despite their history of human sacrifice and their other cruel ceremonies, were cannier than many other tribes. Their contempt and hate for the white man did not stop them from working with him when they felt it suited their purposes, as they did when they aided the French in raiding Spanish settlements in the Southwest. But while they would deal with the white man when they wanted to do so, they'd also massacre the white settlers with the same self-serving impunity. Canyon had never thought well of the Pawnee, as he never thought well of those who made honor a matter of convenience.

Canyon sent the horse south, where the land rose in a long, low hillock, and rode till dusk began to slide its way slowly across the land. He found a cluster of honey locust, just about at the western end of the tree's range, he estimated. He unsaddled the palomino for the night. He ate a few strips of dried beef, undressed as the night stayed warm, and stretched out on a blanket under the long, flat, reddish-brown seedpods, some almost a foot long, that hung from the ornamental, compound leaves. The ivory-gripped Colt at his side, he closed his eyes and let his thoughts turn back to beginnings, the reasons that brought him to this Kansas Territory.

The city came into his mind first: Washington, the nation's capital, and then the great white house with its four, tall columns forming the central part of the facade. He saw himself inside then, where James Buchanan, the fifteenth president of the nation, had had the entire interior renovated, installing American-made furniture for the work of French craftsmen. Canyon saw himself in one of the paneled rooms, a cherry-wood desk in front of him as he faced the tall man with silver-white hair that rose into an unruly tuft just over his forehead.

President Buchanan, his head carried slightly to one side, a characteristic of the man, offered a wide, gracious smile. "Good to see you again, Agent

O'Grady," the president had said. "I'm glad they've picked my favorite government agent for this one."

"Thanks, Mr. President," Canyon had said. He and James Buchanan shared a common heritage, both coming from the green hills and dark moors of Ireland.

"I'm going to have Bill Tardun brief you on this one, O'Grady," the president said. "As my chief aide, he's been handling this very delicate business from the beginning. He's the man to spell it out for you."

"Very good," Canyon said, and watched the man come into the room, a thin file folder in one hand. Canyon had dealt with Bill Tardun before and knew him to be a thorough man, if a little stuffy.

As the president walked from the room with a last wave, his aide seated himself behind the big desk and opened the file folder. "The president's worried, O'Grady," Tardun said. "It's all this talk in the southern states about secession."

"I've heard some of it. I keep wondering if it's nothing more than talk," Canyon said.

"Where there's smoke, there's fire," the official said. "Of course, we don't think there'll be much more than talk until we see whether Mr. Lincoln or Mr. Douglas will be the next president."

"That's not so far away." Canyon nodded.

"That's why we're worried. We've heard that some of the secessionist leaders have been making military plans. We hear they've named Robert E. Lee and Pierre Beauregard to top command posts."

"It's still rumor and talk," Canyon said.

"True, but the president decided Washington can't afford to take it lightly. We've decided to stockpile silver," Tardun said. "Paper currency is only as strong as the government issuing it. It can become worthless overnight unless it's backed by hard assets. Silver will stay a base for buying anything we might need even if we have currency problems. We've already begun the process of stockpiling silver."

Canyon's brow took on a small furrow. "How does this bring me into it?" he asked.

"We have miners bring the silver to an army depot. From there, it's taken by wagon to a secret storage place where it's kept under heavy guard," Tardun said. "But as regularly as we send out the shipments, they're raided along the way. So far only a few chests have been taken in each raid, but we're afraid a major raid will happen one day and make off with an entire shipment. We can't afford that. It seems plain that somebody inside is tipping off the raiders as to when and where the shipments are being moved."

"That's my job: to find out who it is and put a stop to the raids before you lose a major shipment," Canyon said, and the president's aide nodded gravely.

"You'll go to the depot and start there," Tardun said. "The shipments from the depot are handled by an army road agent. You're familiar with the position of a road agent, of course."

"He's a civilian contracted by the army to handle anything and everything the government wants shipped," Canyon said. "Clothing, supplies, spare parts, guns, ammunition, boxed beef or cattle on the hoof, whatever. A good road agent knows the territory, the haulage outfits, the markets, and the people, including the Indians. And I know they're supposed to save the government a lot of money doing things it'd cost three times as much for the army to do, besides tying up personnel."

Tardun fixed him with a probing glance. "But it sounds as though you don't really like road agents," he said.

"Let's say I've met too many who were busy cheating everybody except themselves," Canyon answered.

"We don't feel Jake Sanderson is one of that kind. We've used him for some time now," Tardun said. "Nonetheless, all he knows is that we're sending an expert gunhand and scout to protect our silver shipments." He reached over and handed Canyon a small square of paper. "Directions for finding the depot. It's at the base of the Flint Hills in the Kansas Territory. Good luck, Agent O'Grady."

Canyon rose, shook the hand Tardun extended, and strode from the room. . . .

The mind pictures went blank with that, and Canyon stretched on the blanket, grimaced as he frowned up into the deep blue of the night sky. Someone had known he'd been on the way and had an ambush waiting to end his mission before it started. Someone from where? Canyon pondered. From the army depot at the base of Flint Hills? Or from the capital? Washington was a city where secrets seldom stayed secret for very long. He hadn't left the capital right away, he reminded himself. He'd taken a day to gather his own things and another day for a set of new shoes on the palomino. There were never enough smithies in Washington for all the horses there. So there'd been enough time for a hard-riding messenger to reach Kansas before him and prepare an ambush, Canyon decided.

One of the four dry-gulchers had gotten away, Canyon recalled. Had he simply fled? Or had he raced to report failure? Perhaps he was still waiting somewhere, hoping to finish the job. Maybe payment depended on success. That arrangement was common enough among those who hired killers. The possibility was too real to ignore, Canyon told himself as he closed his eyes and let sleep chase away further speculation.

The night remained quiet and he slept well and rose with the new day. He was in the saddle as the sun cleared the low hills, heading due west. He rode with one hand on the butt of the big Colt at his hip, and his eyes scanned each line of trees that he neared. The flat prairie had given way to gentle hills with plenty of shagbark hickory, silver maple, and black oak, and he slowed his pace. He was too easy a target in the open, he decided, and he moved into the edge of the tree cover. When a line of trees ended and open space followed, he sent the palomino into a gallop till he rode into the next tree cover.

He had just reached a stand of hickory when he heard the shot, followed by two more. He reined to a halt just as he saw a rider burst into the open along the top of a slope. Four near-naked horsemen chased after him on sturdy, saddleless Indian ponies. Two of the pursuers chased the man while the other two raced toward the bottom of the slope to cut him off.

Pawnee, Canyon saw, very young braves, but still with the large heads and heavy faces of the Pawnee. A design on the armband of one was only a confirmation. The fleeing rider drew closer and Canyon swore softly as he saw the green kerchief around the man's neck. He was the last dry-gulcher and he'd probably been riding the hills, looking for another chance at finishing the job, when the Pawnee came onto him.

There was a certain poetic justice to it. Canyon half-smiled as he stayed in the trees and watched. The Pawnee were boxing the man in. He fired off another two shots, all wild, and the Indians stayed flattened on their ponies. The man tried to wheel and cut back up the hill, the move a mistake as his horse hadn't enough power or speed left. The Pawnee closed in on their quarry with wild shouts, and for a moment the dry-gulcher disappeared from sight. Then Canyon saw him on the ground, the four braves standing around him. O'Grady saw the dry-gulcher's horse running on down the slope as two of the Pawnee leapt to the ground and yanked the man to his feet. They wrapped a length of rawhide around his neck. Returning to their ponies, they began to drag the man behind them up the slope.

When they disappeared down the other side of the ridge, Canyon moved from the trees and rode to the top of the slope. The four braves were moving leisurely, dragging their captive behind them, and Canyon's eyes narrowed. He held no sympathy for the dry-gulcher and ordinarily he'd let the Indians do what they wanted with him. But the man had answers he wanted to hear, Canyon mused. His worthless hide might be worth saving for that. The four braves were moving toward the Flint Hills with their captive. They were apparently going to take him to their camp, no doubt to let everyone enjoy his screams. The Indians and their prisoner would leave a trail easy to follow, and Canyon turned the palomino back down the slope.

If he decided to try to save the dry-gulcher for himself, he'd need something to bargain with. The horse might just do it, Canyon decided. The four braves were young and careless, too eager to return with a captive to parade before the camp. The chief would have very little approval if he knew they'd left a good horse and other things behind. Canyon rode to the bottom of the hill, picked up the tracks in the warm, soft soil, and found the horse a few hundred yards on, grazing in a field of witchgrass. He came up to the horse, took the animal's reins in hand, and started back, the dry-gulcher's horse in tow. Returning to the other side of the hill, he quickly picked up the tracks of the four Pawnee and their captive and followed after the trail. He drew close enough for an occasional glimpse of them but made certain to stay far enough back and downwind.

The Neosho River came into sight where it ran along the baseline of the Flint Hills, and Canyon saw the Pawnee cross at a point where the water was not much more than a wide stream at this dry season. His instructions directed him to find the Neosho and go south along the west bank until he reached the army depot. But the Pawnee went directly into the Flint Hills, and Canyon continued to follow. He waited and made certain they were well out of sight before he rode into the open to cross the road. On the other side, he picked up the tracks again and drew close enough once more to keep them in sight. Tree cover grew heavier as they rode into the hills, and Canyon heard the dry-gulcher crying out in exhaustion. He fell to his knees at one point only to be yanked to his feet and half-dragged, half-pulled along.

Canyon estimated they had gone perhaps a mile deeper into the hills, the forest staying thick. He had drawn a dozen yards closer when suddenly his nostrils twitched. He reined to a halt, drew in another deep breath, and the scent was there again, unmistakable, smoky fires drying out meat.

Canyon moved on after the Pawnee once more and caught the sounds of voices drifting through the woods. He slowed, stopped again, and tethered the dry-gulcher's horse to a low branch and moved forward on the palomino. The voices grew louder, more excited, sudden shouts. The four Pawnee had entered the camp with their captive.

Canyon went on carefully until suddenly the camp came into view. His eyes swept a long, cleared area. No hunting camp, he saw at once, but a full base camp with plenty of squaws, tepees, racks for drying meat and pounding skins. He stayed in the saddle and edged still closer. He could see the entire camp plainly now.

The four young braves paraded their captive in front of the rest of the braves and squaws who gathered around, finally halting outside a tepee set apart from the others with a gray-white front panel. A figure stepped from the tepee and the others grew silent. Canyon took in the man, saw the lone golden eagle's feather in his long black hair and the necklace of polished stones that hung against his bare chest. He also saw a large, hooked nose on a heavy face and a well-muscled body. The man was tall for a Pawnee and plainly the chief.

Still not close enough to catch words, Canyon watched the young braves tell their chief of the capture of the white man. From their gestures, they were plainly embellishing the story. Canyon glanced at the dry-gulcher. The man was on his knees, still held by the length of rawhide around his now-raw neck, and his face was a mask of terror.

But he was still the only avenue to the questions O'Grady wanted answered, and he was still alive, though it was anyone's guess how long he'd stay that way. "It's worth a try," Canyon whispered to the palomino as he let thoughts race through his mind. The Pawnee spoke the Caddoan language, but most knew enough of the more widely spoken Siouan which the Crow, Osage, Dakota, and the old Kansa spoke. Canyon had learned his Siouan well—and long ago, he reminded himself confidently—and he knew the universal sign language well. He'd make himself understood, he was certain.

He moved the palomino forward. "A little boldness adds spice to life," he murmured, and rode from the trees to halt at the edge of the Pawnee camp. He waited, let the horse snort, and saw the nearest braves turn to stare at him in openmouthed surprise. Others, hearing their murmurs of astonishment, turned to see him until the entire camp watched him slowly move the horse forward. They parted for him as he moved forward to halt before the chief. He dismounted and faced the man's frowning, incredulous stare. Canyon felt the quivering inside his stomach, but he kept his jaw tight. To show any fear would be fatal, he knew, and he silently reminded himself of the fact.

He spoke in Siouan and accompanied his words with sign language as he pointed to the dry-gulcher. "He is mine. He is my prisoner. I was chasing him when your braves took him," he conveyed. The chief stared at him, his heavy face expressionless. Canyon touched his own chest with one finger. "Canyon O'Grady," he said, and repeated the name again and waited, let his eyes boldly demand a reply.

"Thunderstone, Chief of the Flint Hills Pawnee," the Indian said.

Canyon nodded and gestured to the dry-gulcher on his knees. "I want him," he said.

The Pawnee chief's eyes became tiny chips of black coal as he surveyed the tall man in front of him. "You have fire in your hair," the chief said. "And a fool inside your body."

Canyon had his answers ready. This was the delicate part. The Pawnee enjoyed outwitting the white man almost more than killing him. "I will trade for him," Canyon said.

Chief Thunderstone frowned. "Trade what?" he said, using sign language.

"His horse and all his things with it," Canyon said. "Your braves lied to you. There was no battle and they let his horse run away."

The chief's eyes were stone as they went to the

braves. He bit out questions in the Caddoan tongue, but their meaning was crystal-clear and Canyon saw the braves shrug, then nod sullenly. The chief returned his coal-black eyes to the big man with the hair of flame. "I will trade this worthless thing for the horse and everything with it," he said.

Canyon touched his heart, the gesture common in all sign language. "A pact of honor," he said.

The Pawnee chief touched a finger to his own heart. Canyon nodded. It was done, as best as he could hope for, he knew. He swung onto the palomino, walked the horse slowly through the camp and into the woods. He retrieved the dry-gulcher's horse and returned with it, once again moving slowly, deliberately through the camp. He halted and handed the reins to the chief, who, with an almost imperceptible flicker of his eyelids, nodded toward the dry-gulcher.

Canyon took the length of rawhide and yanked the man to his feet. He led his prisoner through the camp and into the woods, kept a slow pace until he was perhaps a quarter-mile away from the camp.

"Get this thing off my neck, will you?" the man said, and O'Grady tossed the rawhide down and waited as the man pulled himself loose. "Thanks for back there," the dry-gulcher said. "I owe you one."

"And you're going to pay it right now, you miserable son of a bitch," Canyon said, and swung down from the palomino. "Who told you to dry-gulch me?" he asked. "You talk or you'll be as dead as if I'd left you with the Pawnee, only quicker."

He saw the man's eyes start to grow crafty. "What happens to me if I tell you?" the man asked.

"It's what'll happen to you if you don't talk that you'd best worry about," Canyon growled.

The man swallowed hard. "All right," he muttered. They were his last words: the arrow, fired at full force, struck him in the back and the arrowhead came out through the front of his chest. His mouth opened as he fell forward, but Canyon was already flinging himself sideways and heard the second arrow whistle past his head. He landed on his side, the Colt in his hand, saw one of the young braves start to leap over a log toward him. He fired from his side and the Indian's abdomen exploded in red as he pitched forward.

Canyon rolled as another arrow plowed into the ground; he came up shooting and caught another of the four young braves racing at him. This time his shot spun the Pawnee almost completely around as it smashed into the left part of his chest. The two other young braves, fury in their faces, were rushing at him with nasty hide-scraping knives in their hands.

They came in a furious rush. Canyon had time to level the Colt at only one, and he chose the hurtling form to the right, fired, and didn't wait to see the man go down as he twisted sideways and felt the edge of the knife graze his shoulder.

The Pawnee was young and quick. He struck out with a hard backhanded blow that caught Canyon on his elbow, and Canyon felt the Colt fly from his hand. The Indian was atop him instantly, one arm with the jagged-edged blade upraised to bring it down. O'Grady managed to get his left hand up, close it around the Indian's wrist, and deflect the blow as it crashed down. He twisted, used the leverage of the man's own body, and heard the man grunt in pain. Canyon hurled his shoulder into the Pawnee's thigh and his attacker went down on one knee. Ignoring the sharp pain still in his elbow, he brought a short, right uppercut onto the point of the brave's chin. The Indian fell back and the knife dropped from his hand. Canyon reached for the weapon where it lay on the ground, closed one hand around it, and had begun to bring the blade up when the Pawnee hurled himself forward. Canyon managed to turn the blade around as the Indian slammed into him. He felt the jagged edge tear deeply into the man's abdomen.

He drew his hand back as the brave staggered, and he saw the jagged slash across the Pawnee's abdomen that already spilled uneven lines of red down the man's body. The Indian clasped one hand to the deep wound, staggered again and fell to one knee, swayed for another moment, and collapsed onto the ground. Canyon pushed to his feet, and his eyes went to the dry-gulcher's lifeless body, the arrow embedded in it almost to the feathers.

"Damn," Canyon swore. He turned away, swallowed the frustrated anger, and climbed onto the saddle. The four braves had slipped from camp in sullen anger, he was almost certain, but he wanted to see for himself. He turned the horse back to the Pawnee camp. The silence fell over the camp again when he rode in and Thunderstone stepped from his tepee as Canyon halted.

"Your word was from the heart, a pledge of honor," Canyon said, and used sign language again to emphasize his words.

"It was so," Thunderstone said, his face severe.

"Your braves came. They killed my prisoner," Canyon said, and saw the flicker of surprise pass over the chief's impassive face. "Then they tried to kill me."

"That was wrong. They will be punished," Thunderstone said.

"They have been punished," Canyon answered, the unsaid in the grimness of his eyes as he met the chief's stare.

Thunderstone remained expressionless, but he understood the message in the big, fire-haired man's eyes. His nod, when it came, was a movement so spare as to be hardly noticeable. But Canyon grunted and turned the horse away. He rode slowly from the camp and put the palomino into a trot only when he was in the woods.

He had been right about the four braves, he was certain now. They had slipped from the camp on their own to avenge being humiliated. The moment of surprise in the Pawnee chief's face had confirmed that. He hadn't broken the pledge. Not this time, Canyon grunted. But he'd still not trust a Pawnee. Never.

Yet, as he rode, O'Grady found himself wondering at his own actions. Had he returned to the Pawnee chief solely to confirm his own suspicions about the four braves? That had been the surface of it, of course. But had there been more? Had he wanted to establish a line to the Pawnee? If so, why? he asked himself, and had no answers. Why? The question danced. Some called such things the result of inner voices. Premonitions? Undefined yet still there? Harbingers closeted deep in the inner mind? Perceptions of the soul we can neither understand nor recognize nor explain? He never rejected such things, Canyon grunted. He had seen too much beyond explaining on purely rational, conscious terms.

He shook away thoughts with a touch of irritation. Those were musings made for a glass of fine port beside a good fire. He had no business wasting time with such now. There were hard, practical matters that lay ahead, and he emerged from the woods, put the pale-bronze horse into a fast trot, and made his way back to the Neosho River. He turned and followed the bank as the river ran along the baseline of the Flint Hills.

The sun was in the midafternoon sky when the handful of low frame buildings came into sight in the distance. It was time to play the role assigned to him. Carefully.

3

The army depot turned out to be a small collection of wood structures with a barrack building to one side that could hardly accommodate half a platoon. As he rode up, Canyon saw a dozen or so troopers lounging about and eight wagons lined up along one side of the area, unhitched and waiting. They were mostly Owensboro mountain wagons, rear wheels larger than the front, with the body style often called California rack bed. Each rig held a generous supply of canvas coverings. A low, oblong, open-faced building seemed to be a modest trading post, and beside it, a square, shacklike structure bore a sign that read OFFICE.

Canyon halted and swung to the ground.

The man who came from the office seemed as large as the building. "O'Grady," he said. "Expected you a few days ago."

"Had some delays," Canyon said.

"Jake Sanderson," the huge man said with a grin. "They told me you were redheaded. They were sure right."

Jake Sanderson had a wide and round, fleshy face that fitted his body, which had to weigh near three hundred pounds, Canyon guessed. Too much fat on it, but a lot of muscle beneath the fat; arms that resembled small trees, a chest of massive proportions, and a head that seemed to sit on his shoulders with no neck in between. Sanderson had thinning brown hair that he combed flat to one side, and his eyes seemed smaller than they were in the folds of the wide, fleshy face.

"Got some bad news for you, O'Grady. I know Washington sent you to scout and ride gun for me, and they said you were real good. But I'm not going to be needing you, not for some while." Canyon's brow creased in a frown instantly. "The next shipment's been canceled."

"Canceled?" Canyon echoed in surprise.

"Problems at the silver mine," Sanderson said.

"Washington know about this?"

"Sent them a messenger yesterday, soon as I found out," Jake Sanderson said, and shrugged apologetically.

"How long will the next shipment be delayed?" Canyon queried.

"Can't say for sure. I'd guess at least a month, maybe two," the huge man said. He offered a frown of sympathy. "Now, I know you've come a long way to earn some good money and it's a damn shame."

"It sure is," Canyon said, and let himself appear upset. He couldn't do otherwise and stay in his role. "Hell, I was looking forward to putting a stop to whoever's been raiding the shipments."

"That mightn't be so easy, O'Grady," the man said, and beckoned to him. "Come into the office where we can talk better." He led the way into the small structure where the only pieces of furniture were two hard-backed chairs and a battered wood desk. "They told me you were a sharp-eyed scout and a fine hand with a gun. Hell, I'll take all the help I can get. I've taken every precaution I know and we're still being raided."

"Such as?" Canyon questioned.

"Changing crews every trip. I start out here with a

crew of drivers and guards, pay them off when we reach the storage base, and hire a new crew for the next trip, all to make sure nobody gets to know the route too well. Now, if that's not taking precautions, I don't know what is.''

"But they still manage to raid you," Canyon said.

"As I keep telling Washington, the raiders have been plumb lucky, that's all.''

"How many wagons go on a shipment?" Canyon asked.

"From three to five, a driver for each and four shotgun riding guards.''

"I was told they've only taken a chest or a few small boxes in these raids. Why? Why didn't they just make off with the whole shipment?''

"Because they aren't equipped to make off with more than a chest or a few boxes. These varmints are strictly small-time, nothing more," Sanderson said.

Canyon turned the answer in his mind. It didn't completely satisfy him, but he decided against pressing further on it.

"This is strictly isolated stuff, raids by a few bands of hill bandits. They're happy to get away with a chest of silver.''

"You're saying it's not always the same band," Canyon suggested.

Jake Sanderson nodded. "That's right. There've been two or three. I see this as strictly isolated raids by a few hill bandits.''

"You ever consider there's a leak from someplace here?" Canyon asked. "Maybe even one of the troopers?''

"Thought about it. Can't see it. Nobody knows when I'm taking a shipment out except me. But that's another reason why I get a new crew each trip. Nobody gets a chance to get too familiar with anything I do.''

"I guess you'd know about that,'' Canyon said agreeably while the reservations still held inside him.

Sanderson went around to the other side of the old battered desk, opened a drawer, and took out a small envelope. "But all this doesn't help you any, O'Grady. It's still no job and no money for you, and none of it your fault. I'm going to help you out.''

Canyon's brow lifted in interest. "You've some other wagons for me to scout for?'' he asked.

"No. It's personal, but I'll pay you whatever Washington is paying you and that'll make up for the cancellation,'' the man said expansively.

"Well, now, that's right fair of you,'' Canyon said with the right mixture of gratitude and defense. "Personal, you said?''

"That's right. I want you to find my wife and bring her back,'' Jake Sanderson said. "She ran off with a smooth-talking drummer last week. A fancy line of talk always impressed her.''

"And fancy talk is what a salesman does best,'' Canyon agreed.

"Damn right. I imagine it'll take a while to find her and that damn drummer. By the time you do and then bring her back to me, the next shipment ought to be ready to roll,'' Jake Sanderson said. "How about it, O'Grady?''

Canyon let himself think for a moment, but he knew he really had no choice. He couldn't get a handle on the big man in front of him, not so quickly. Maybe Sanderson was genuinely concerned and sympathetic and saw a chance to get his wife back at the same time. But one thing was certain: he couldn't turn down the offer. It would be out of character for a hired hand suddenly faced with no job. It'd almost certainly make

Sanderson wonder about him and he didn't want that. But there was one more reason: Sanderson's wife had run off, but she might just know a good deal about the activities at the depot.

Canyon brought his eyes back to the huge man. "I'm grateful and I thank you," he said.

"You just bring her back and I'll be thanking you," Jake Sanderson said. "I still want her, despite her running off that way."

"Got any idea where they might've headed?"

"Into the Flint Hills. That damn drummer trades with the Indians and he'd figure that'd be a good place to hide," Sanderson said. "Her name's Blueberry and she's a good-looking peach blond."

"I'll do my best. I'm no tracker, though," Canyon said. "I know a man, Fargo, they call him the Trailsman. If he were here, I could do it. He can track a fly on ice."

"Do your best. I'd have gone after her myself but I was waiting for that shipment and now I can't just up and leave things here," Sanderson said.

"I'll be starting right away. There's enough day left to ride a ways," Canyon said.

Sanderson drew a fistful of bills from his shirt pocket and handed them to the big, flame-haired man. "Half in advance," he said. "Good luck, O'Grady."

Canyon nodded and Sanderson watched him walk from the tiny office. Outside, Canyon climbed onto the palomino and rode away. He held a steady trot that quickly left the depot behind. He swung onto a narrow road along the base of the Flint Hills. He let a sigh blow from his lips as he patted the pale-bronze neck of the horse. " 'Nature hath framed strange fellows in her time,' so said Will Shakespeare," Canyon remarked. "True, very true, Cormac, lad, and Jake Sanderson may well be one of them. He may be a man of real sympathy and feeling, or he may be a royal rascal. My senses tell me he's not what he seems to be, but he's put me in a truss, for the moment, at least." The palomino snorted and shook his blond mane. "Agreed, then, is it?" Canyon laughed. "The shipment being canceled has put a new face on things. Chances are I'd not learn much waiting around the depot, so this may actually be the best of a bad turn."

He patted the powerful neck again and lapsed into silence. But his thoughts continued to tumble after one another and they turned to Blueberry Sanderson and her traveling salesman. If they'd gone straight into the hills, there was damn little chance he'd find them except by sheer luck. But there were a few settlements along the base of the hills, none large enough to deserve being called a town. Yet there was a good chance that the couple might have stopped at one of them, if only to rest a spell, before taking on the hills. He'd try there first, Canyon decided. But the night slid down from the hills before he reached the first settlement and he drew the palomino into a cluster of white ash and found a soft spot to bed down. The night stayed warm, and as he undressed and stretched out on his blanket, Jake Sanderson swam back into his idle thoughts.

The man had talked openly. He had detailed his precautions, explained his thinking, and generally made his points well. He seemed convinced the raids had been carried out by random groups of mountain bandits. Only one thing refused to hold up: why did the bandits make off with only a chest at a time? The question still hung in his thoughts. Because they were small-time bandits not ready to carry off anything more, Sanderson had insisted. Canyon rejected that answer. They could have made off with the wagons and all the silver in them. But they hadn't, not in any of the raids. Why? It just didn't make sense. He didn't accept Sanderson's explanation. Yet he had no better one, Canyon admitted. But there had to be another explanation beside the one Sanderson offered: he was certain of that much. Canyon frowned. It was perhaps the only thing of which he was certain. Sanderson, for all his apparent openness, was a large question mark. Canyon let speculation drift away, closed his eyes, and embraced sleep.

When morning came with a hot sun, he woke, washed with his canteen, and dressed. He breakfasted on a stand of wild plums and rode along the baseline of the hills to finally come to the first settlement. He saw a low-roofed saloon surrounded by a small trading shack, a smithy, and a barbershop. A long supply storage shed made up the rest of the settlement, and Canyon brought the palomino to a halt outside the trading shack. A thin-faced man looked out from an open front to the shack where a dozen pelts hung from a hook and an equal number of Indian blankets were stacked on the counter.

"Mornin', traveler," the man said.

"And a good morning to you," Canyon replied.

"Want to buy, sell, or trade?" the man asked.

"Neither. I'm looking for a young woman and a man riding with her. She's a peach blond, attractive, name's Blueberry," Canyon said.

The thin man straightened up and shouted into the back of the trading shack. "Sam, get out here," he called, excitement in his voice, and Canyon saw a figure appear inside the shack, come forward, and take form as a bearded man walking with one crutch, his left foot and ankle wrapped in thick bandages. "This here feller's lookin' for that damn Blueberry gal," the thin man said.

The man with the bandaged foot hobbled forward

and his face darkened. "What do you want with her, mister?"

"A man paid me to find her and bring her back," Canyon said.

"I'll give you fifty dollars if you bring her to me, the damn bitch," the man roared. "This hobbling I'm doing is her damn fault."

Canyon's brows lifted. "Want to fill in the whole of it?" he said, and the man's frowning face remained darkened in anger.

"She came riding up and wanted to buy a rifle. It was near dark and I've a room in back I rent out to travelers. She agreed she might stay the night, but she wanted the rifle first. I had a good lever-action Volcanic I offered her for twenty dollars. She said she wouldn't pay more than ten for it. One word led to another. She's a rotten-tongued little bitch, said I was tryin' to cheat her. She took the rifle, shot me in the foot, left ten dollars, and ran off."

"What about the man with her?" Canyon questioned.

"There was nobody with her when she stopped here," the man said.

"You sure?" Canyon frowned.

"Damn right I'm sure."

"You know which way she ran off?" Canyon queried.

"Straight into the hills just behind my place. She just up and took off like a jackrabbit with my rifle, damn her bitchy hide," the man said.

"Much obliged," Canyon said. "I'll be going on after her."

"Abe Zeller has his trap lines straight up into the hills. Maybe he's seen her," the man said.

"I'll look for him," Canyon said.

"Fifty dollars to bring the little bitch back to me, mister," the man called out again.

Canyon nodded as he sent the palomino past the trading shack and into the hills. He found a narrow pathway up and took it until it came to an end and he had to move up across the hills. He spotted a good stand of box elder just made for trapping, and caught the glint of sun on a stream that wandered into the thick woodlands. He turned the horse and rode into the trees, found the stream again, and peered through the woods as he followed the narrow, winding course of the water.

He frowned in thought as he rode. Blueberry Sanderson had been alone, the trader had said, and that didn't fit either. Perhaps the drummer had hung back, but Canyon couldn't find a reason for that. Unless the man had thought Blueberry could get a better buy on a rifle if she appeared alone. That was a piece of pure speculation, yet it was a possibility. He tucked the thought away in his mind as the stream made a sudden turn and he spotted a trap line along one bank. He saw a nasty, big-toothed trap half-hidden by leaves.

Abe Zeller was an efficient but careless trapper. A good trapper was more careful where he put a number-one bear trap that could snap a horse's leg as though it were a straw.

Canyon skirted the trap and rode on, staying away from the edge of the stream as he spotted another trap. He rode on, smelled the odor of a wood fire, and turned the horse to follow it until he spied a small hut, trapper's gear scattered around the open door. A gray-bearded, thin man stepped from the hut as Canyon rode up, his left arm bandaged and held in a home-made sling. The man held a heavy Remington-Beals Army revolver in his right hand, a six-shot single-action weapon with a brass trigger guard.

"You Abe Zeller?" Canyon asked. "The man at the trading shop told me you were up in these parts."

"I'm Abe Zeller," the trapper said.

"You always come to the door with a six-gun in hand?" Canyon asked.

"I though maybe it was that goddamned girl coming back," Zeller said.

"What girl?" Canyon asked, but was instantly certain he already knew the answer.

"That goddamn little blond. See this arm of mine? That was her doing," Zeller exploded.

"What happened?" Canyon asked.

"She came riding up here, said she was trying to find some wagon tracks and had I seen any this way," the trapper said. "Before I could answer, she saw a doe I'd caught in a snare trap a half-dozen yards back of the hut. The damn deer was strung up by one leg where she'd stepped into the snare. I told her the deer had only been hanging there a few hours."

"Still alive, I take it."

The man nodded. "I was going to take the damn doe down when I got around to it," he muttered.

"What'd she do, then?" Canyon asked.

"First she called me all kinds of names. Then she pushed this big old Smith and Wesson rifle in my face and told me to cut the doe loose. I did it and then she set the snare again, made me put my arm in it, and sprang it. I was hanging by one arm for half the day before I managed to get loose," the trapper said. "My damn arm's still all pulled out of shape."

"And she just rode off," Canyon said, and the man nodded as he spat. "I was told she was traveling with a man," Canyon added.

"Not when she was here. She was all by her damn self," the trapper said. "Was only yesterday. You can probably pick up her tracks, but why in hell anyone would want to find her is past me.''

"Got a job to do," Canyon said, and he urged the palomino past the trapper's hut and on into the woods.

Abe Zeller had been right about picking up her hoofprints; Canyon easily found the tracks of the lone horse and rider. He followed a trail that seemed to wander aimlessly through the woodlands. Blueberry Sanderson was fast becoming a most unusual young woman. What was she doing searching the mountains for wagon tracks? Canyon wondered. She was apparently alone. What had happened to the drummer she'd run away with? Had she ditched him as soon as she was free of Jake Sanderson? Maybe she was a thoroughly self-centered little package who used men as stepping-stones. But her reaction to the doe didn't fit that sort of personality.

He was still thinking about the young woman when the tracks led out of the woods and across a slope with thin tree cover. He found where she had bedded down for the night and then gone on in the morning. Her tracks were fresh, not more than a few hours old. But she continued to wander from one side of the hills to the other, plainly searching for the wagon tracks she'd asked the trapper about. The pursuit of Blueberry Sanderson grew stranger by the hour. She had steered her horse across a ridge, then down the other side, and wandered into a high valley and out again.

O'Grady saw a pattern of wagons tracks that she came onto, but they were weeks old and seemed to wind their way to no place. But Canyon's frown deepened as he halted to carefully examine the tracks. More than one wagon, though the wheels followed in the same ruts. As many as six wagons, perhaps, he guessed, certainly four. Jake Sanderson's wagons, he wondered. He moved on again after the horse's hoofprints.

She had wandered back and forth through the low hills, and the night began to slide over the land when the prints turned higher into the hills. Canyon also noted a few lines of unshod pony prints. He finally had to bed down as darkness descended, certain he'd catch up to the young woman in the morning. He ate some pemmican from his saddlebag and quickly embraced sleep until the new day's sun woke him with a warm caress. He was in the saddle, tracking the hoofprints again, before the sun finished rising above the tops of the hills, and he muttered under his breath as her trail turned downhill again.

The first set of wagon tracks had disappeared in the ground and she plainly searched for another set. The sun was hanging high in the noon sky when he came onto her, the horse first, standing alone near a small pond. His eyes swept the pond and found the young woman, peach-blond hair glistening in the sun as she finished buttoning a white shirt. She had obviously just finished a dip in the pond, her hair still wet.

"Poor timing, lad," Canyon murmured to himself. He watched the young woman walk toward her horse, halt, and slide down to rest against a tree trunk. He guided the palomino in a half-circle that brought him behind her, slid to the ground, and moved forward on foot. She was deep in her own thoughts and completely unaware of his presence. He saw a rounded figure as he drew closer, broad shoulders, and when she suddenly rose to her feet, full breasts and a round rear with sturdy legs under a brown riding skirt. She had a pretty-enough face, a small nose with a pugnacious chin and full red lips that seemed ready to pout.

Her peach-blond hair hung straight and full around

her face, brushed back from a smooth forehead. When she turned toward her horse, he saw bright-blue eyes.

Canyon stepped into the open and she halted at once to stare at him in surprise. She started toward the rifle hanging from its shoulder strap on the saddle, and Canyon took a step closer, the Colt in his hand instantly. "Don't, lassie," he said.

She stopped and he saw no fear in her eyes, only a belligerent frown touching her brow. "What do you want?" she said crisply. "Who are you?"

"Canyon O'Grady," the big man said. "I'm not here to harm you."

"That's nice," she said laconically, and Canyon smiled. She wasn't one for being easily rattled.

"I've come to fetch you back, nothing more," Canyon said.

The young woman's frown grew deeper and she put her hands on her hips as she let her eyes move over his handsomely roguish face. "Fetch me back where?" she asked.

"To your husband, Jake Sanderson," Canyon said. "He sent me after you, Blueberry."

Her full red lips parted and a short gasp accompanied the astonishment in her face. "What?" she hissed.

"Even though you ran off with that drummer. He's a forgiving man," Canyon said.

"He's a damn liar. He's not my husband. He never was and never would be."

"And you didn't run away with a smooth-talking traveling salesman?"

"No, dammit."

"And you're not Blueberry Sanderson?" Canyon pressed childingly.

"My name's Blueberry Hill," the young woman

said. "My ma had a sense of humor." She glared belligerently at him as he peered at her.

"And you didn't shoot that trader, Sam, in the foot?" Canyon pressed. "And take off with that rifle?"

Her angry frown softened for a moment. "Yes, I did that. I suppose that's all he told you."

"Such as?"

"That he rented me the room for the night but didn't tell me he came with it. I told him to get out when he came calling. When he had other ideas, I shot him in the foot. He was lucky. I could've shot him someplace else," Blueberry sniffed.

"What about the trapper?"

"That cruel bastard. I told him to cut that doe down, and he laughed at me. He's even luckier than the other slob. I was thinking of putting his neck in that snare. I settled for his arm," she said. "Trapping's cruel enough. You don't have to make it worse. His kind deserve a taste of their own medicine."

Canyon felt the frown crease his own brow. There was more than enough anger to her, but he saw no guile, no attempt at sidestepping anything. "You'll admit you have cut quite a path on your way up here," he said.

She shrugged, the gesture pure dismissal. "I'm still not married to that fat slob," she snapped.

"So you keep insisting."

"And you don't believe me."

Canyon started to reply and found himself surprised at his hesitation. He took another moment to pull his own thoughts together. "I can't say that," he admitted honestly. "But I can't say I do, either."

"Use your common sense. You don't think I'd marry a big, fat, ugly slob like Jake Sanderson, do you?" Blueberry threw back.

"Now, that logic won't hold up, girl. I've seen many a beautiful woman married up to an ugly man." Canyon laughed. "There are all kinds of reasons for marrying, as every woman knows."

She glowered back. "No matter, he's not my husband. You can believe me or not. I don't care."

Canyon met her angry glower as thoughts still whirled inside him. "You're full of brass and sass, I'll say that," he remarked. "But I'll still be taking you back."

"Anything to earn your money?" she accused.

"I agreed to do a job. I'm going to do it."

"Even if he lied to you about me?" Blueberry pressed.

"I can't decide the truth of that here. There's too much hanging in midair."

"Such as?"

"Why would he send me to fetch you back if he weren't your husband?"

"I don't know why he sent you," Blueberry returned angrily.

"Then I guess I'll not find the truth of it till we get back," Canyon said. "Now, we can have a pleasant ride back or an unpleasant one. That'll be up to you, Blueberry."

"I wouldn't think of upsetting you by being unpleasant," she said disdainfully.

"That's good," Canyon said calmly. He took the rifle from her horse. "I'll be taking this just to help you keep your word. Now let's get my horse." She walked silently beside him to where he'd left the palomino, Cormac, her head high, back straight, full breasts under the white shirt thrusting forward, as bold as the rest of her. "You can mount up, now," he said after he'd climbed onto the palomino.

She let a chiding smile touch the full lips. "You

always this cautious or is it just with dangerous crim-inals?''

"A talent for sarcasm, too." Canyon laughed. "You're quite a package, Blueberry."

"You didn't answer my question," she sniffed, and pulled herself onto the horse.

"Sometimes I'm very cautious, sometimes not at all. Bringing young ladies back to their husbands is something new to me," Canyon said.

"He's not my husband, dammit. Stop saying that," she flung at him.

Canyon studied her again. He was beginning to al-most believe her. The fury of her was no bit of acting, he was certain. "All right, fair enough," he agreed. "Then I'll say that bringing young ladies back to any-one is something new for me."

Blueberry's blue eyes roved over his face, took in the power of his broad shoulders and the charm of his roguish handsomeness. "I imagine that's true enough," she commented.

"Sorry, flattery won't work." Canyon laughed.

"No flattery. Just an observation."

"You can talk while we ride."

"Why? You don't believe anything I say."

"I might. Convince me."

She cast a sidelong glance at him, her bright-blue eyes appraising again. "Let's talk about Canyon O'Grady," she said. "Who are you? How come you came to Jake Sanderson?"

"Washington sent me as an extra gun and scout for the silver shipments," Canyon told her.

Blueberry's eyes narrowed as she surveyed him. "You a gunhand and a scout? You can't sell me that," she sniffed.

"Why not?" He frowned and let indignation wrap itself around him.

"I've seen too many of those. You don't fit the mold," she returned.

Canyon inwardly swore at her intuitive sharpness. "Fit or not, that's what I am," he insisted, and saw her shoulders lift in a shrug of disbelief.

"Then why are you here chasing after me? Why aren't you with the shipment?"

"It was canceled for now, which left me with no job," Canyon said as he led the way down a narrow passage and saw darkness moving in quickly. "Jake Sanderson helped me out by paying me to go after you."

"He's full of good deeds," Blueberry said disdainfully.

"It seems so to me," Canyon said. "And you still say you don't know why he sent me to fetch you back. You're not his wife, not his girlfriend, you're not anything to him, yet you seem to know him well enough to have definite opinions about him."

"I didn't say I didn't know him."

"No, you didn't," Canyon admitted with a smile. "You insist on walking this tightrope, don't you?"

"He gave you a cock-and-bull story about me. I don't know why. That's all I'm going to say."

"We can talk more after we find a spot to bed down," Canyon answered. He hurried the palomino forward until he spotted two red maples that offered privacy and shelter. He found a wide bed of wavy broom moss with its long tendrils forming a glossy mat under the trees, and he slid to the ground and unsaddled the palomino.

Blueberry followed his example and he watched her move with a strong grace in the last moments of the light as she put her saddle against one of the tree trunks.

"You have anything to eat with you?" he asked.

"A few cans in my saddlebag," she said.

He gathered some kindling for a small fire and had the blaze going as night blanketed the hills to close out the rest of the world. He ate his pemmican while she took an opener and a can of beans and beef from her saddlebag. She let the opened can warm by the fire before eating from it, and her peach-blond hair sent out golden glints in the firelight. When she finished eating, she sat back on her elbows and Canyon watched the firelight play across the soft swell of her breasts that pushed up under the white shirt.

"You're much too fine-looking a lass for it," he said, and drew an instant frown.

"For what?" she questioned.

"For playing games with the truth," he said.

"You're much too fine-looking a lad to be a gun-hand and scout for Jake Sanderson," she tossed back.

Canyon smiled in admiration. She had a fast mind to go with her loveliness. And an intuitive doggedness he preferred to turn away. "Let's get some sleep and see how we feel, come morning," he said. "Which brings me to a bothersome question. I'd not be tying you up for the night unless I have to. Will you give me your word not to run if I don't tie you?"

"I told you I'm not going back to Sanderson," Blueberry said with a glower of defiance.

"I guess that answers my question," Canyon said with a note of rue in his voice.

"I guess so," she snapped. "But I don't like sleeping in my clothes. I've nightclothes in my saddlebag. I'd like to change."

"Of course," Canyon said. "A little courtesy always helps any situation."

"Indeed," Blueberry said. He watched her go to the saddle and begin to dig into her saddlebag beside the tree. He turned away and put another piece of kindling on the small fire when her voice broke the silence.

"Turn around very slowly and keep your hand away from your holster," he heard Blueberry say. He obeyed and saw her beside her saddle, facing him with a Colt Paterson pocket pistol, a five-shot single-action weapon formidable at close range. She took a step closer and the pistol didn't waver, he noted. "Very slowly, take your gun from the holster and throw it over here," she said.

Again, he obeyed, lifting the big Colt with two fingers and tossing it on the ground in front of her.

"The price of courtesy," Blueberry said.

"The price of not being careful enough," Canyon corrected.

"No matter." She shrugged. "Turn around."

"I didn't think you were the kind of lass to shoot a man in the back," he said.

"Turn around," she said, and he saw her scoop up his gun as he started to turn his back on her. How badly had he misjudged Blueberry? he found himself wondering. The blow that crashed into the back of his head ended further speculation; red and yellow lights exploded inside him as he fell to the ground. He shook his head and the flashing lights disappeared for an instant only to return again until they suddenly blinked out and there was nothing but the empty void of unconsciousness.

4

He woke to the throbbing first, then the sharp pain in the back of his head when he moved. He lay still again while thoughts fell into place. Blueberry came first, with the pocket pistol in her hand. But she hadn't shot him. He hadn't misjudged her that much, he was grateful to find. But he had been incautious and had paid the price, deservedly. He pushed himself to his feet, shook his head, ignoring the pain of it, and cleared away the last of the cobwebs in his mind.

Blueberry was gone, of course, and his eyes went to the palomino. She'd taken her rifle and his big Henry, too, along with the Colt. He had more than one reason to find the peach-blond little package, he murmured grimly.

The moon had come up, letting him see her hoofprints where she'd raced away. He swung onto the palomino and began to follow the tracks, moving slowly to search them out in the pale light of the moon. He finally had to halt as the moon began to curve into the distant sky and its dim light grew still dimmer. Picking up the prints became impossible.

He found a stout hackberry, slid from the saddle, and sat down against the trunk of the tree. His head still throbbed and he embraced sleep with gratefulness until the morning finally dawned and he woke. When he rose, he realized his head had stopped throbbing though it still hurt to the touch.

He used his canteen to wash and freshen up and took to the saddle again, his eyes picking up the hoofprints with ease now. She had cut across the hills, then turned upward. He found where she had halted to rest. It'd not be easy coming up on her unaware this time, he reminded himself, especially with her carrying all his guns as well as her own. As the tracks grew fresher, he slowed and saw the prints lead alongside a line of tall, thin eastern cottonwoods. He estimated he wasn't more than fifteen minutes behind her.

He slowed again to sweep the terrain ahead with a long, careful survey. The land rose, becoming hard with thin ridges and gulleys, plenty of tree cover on the sides of the ridges. He slowed the palomino to a walk, his eyes on the hoofprints again, and suddenly he felt the crease dig into his brow. Blueberry had suddenly put her horse into a gallop: the prints dug hard and deep into the earth.

He spurred Cormac forward and went into a fast canter, his eyes on the tracks where the hoofprints continued to dig deeply into the ground. She had raced toward the nearest ridge that ran alongside a trench. Something had frightened her, sent her racing away. His eyes swept the ridges for signs of bronzed horsemen, but he saw none. He'd ridden halfway up the side of the ridge when he spotted the new hoofprints that suddenly appeared. They formed a trail from the trees and fell in behind Blueberry's tracks. Horses wearing shoes, Canyon grunted, at least four. That's what had sent Blueberry racing away. He spurred the palomino forward to follow the new tracks as they reached the top of the ridge. They moved along the edge of the trench on the other side. Suddenly the sound of voices came to him.

He slowed, pulled the palomino into the trees as the voices became clear. Staying in the trees, he moved on until he saw the men—five, he counted, four out of the saddle at the edge of the trench, one still on his horse. He moved the palomino onto higher ground until he had a good view of the entire scene. Blueberry's horse was a dozen yards away, and then, at the bottom of the trench—some twelve foot deep he guessed—he spied the shimmer of peach-blond hair. The marks at the edge of the trench, along with Blueberry's rifle and his own Henry laying there, told him what had happened. Her horse had lost footing or bucked and thrown her. She'd landed at the edge of the trench, bounced, lost both rifles, and gone into the trench. The revolvers were probably still in her saddlebag, he grunted. All the guns she'd taken with her would do her absolutely no good now.

His gaze went to the men at the edge of the trench as they shouted down to her; she looked up at them. Two of them lowered a length of lasso down to her and Canyon saw that she held a length of stout branch in one hand and sported a bruise on her cheekbone.

"Now, you climb up here, girlie," one of the men said.

"You want me, you come down and get me," Blueberry threw back.

"We'll be real mad if we have to do that, girlie," one of the men said.

"And I'll bet you'll be real gentlemen if I climb up," Blueberry retorted.

The five men were a scrubby, scruffy lot, in torn and faded outfits, cracked leather on their boots, their faces as worn and harsh as their gear. Some of Jake Sanderson's mountain bandits? Canyon pondered, and turned down the thought. These five didn't look as though they could mount a raid on four or five wagons under guard. These were small-time drifters roaming the hills in search of easy prey, and now they'd found an unexpected bonus. Their voices broke into his thoughts as the man in the saddle barked orders.

"She's not comin' up. Go down and get her, Browder," he said. A thin man with a thin mustache started to slide down the rope they had lowered. He hadn't quite reached the bottom, his feet nearly to the ground, when Canyon saw Blueberry swing the length of branch with both hands. It cracked the man across the ribs and he cried out in pain as he dropped to the ground on hands and knees. He hadn't even had a chance to lift his head before Blueberry smashed the clublike length of branch across the back of his neck and he went down on his face to lay still.

"The little bitch," the man on the horse exploded. "Ben, you and Beezer go down and get her." The two men moved at once, the first one starting to slide down the rope, the second immediately after him. Canyon saw Blueberry, the club of wood raised, ready to smash it into the first of the two men. But the man didn't wait to touch the ground. A little more than halfway down, he let go of the rope and leapt the rest of the distance. He hit the ground on both feet before Blueberry could swing her club; he dived to one side as she rushed at him, and avoided her blow. Meanwhile, the second man had also leapt to the ground and rushed at her as she spun to swing the club at him. He ducked away from her blow and the other man seized her from the back, spun her around, and smashed a blow into her stomach.

Blueberry bent in two and collapsed, and the man yanked the length of branch from her and tossed it aside.

"Bring her up," the man on the horse barked. Canyon watched the two men tie the rope around Blueberry's gasping form while the first man slowly got to his feet. They pulled Blueberry from the trench, the man on the horse dismounting to help, and then the others climbed out.

Blueberry staggered back from a hard slap to the face. "Little bitch," the man snarled. "We're gonna screw your tail off before we get rid of you."

Canyon, his lips a thin line, saw them gather up the rifles as they put Blueberry on her horse. One of them held the horse's reins as they began to ride on, Blueberry between them.

"Damn," Canyon swore in frustration. He hadn't so much as a toothpick for a weapon. Blueberry had seen to that and now she was paying the price for her cleverness. It'd be a harsh, brutal kind of poetic justice, he grunted as he kept pace with the riders and stayed inside the trees. He wouldn't even have the chance to try to save her in the night. These five wouldn't wait that long to enjoy themselves with her.

They rode unhurriedly, exchanging crude anticipations with one another. Blueberry rode with her face drawn tight and refused to show anything but contempt. Her toughness was admirable but it would get her nothing if he couldn't get hold of a gun, Canyon realized grimly.

"That's the only chance, Cormac, lad," he said to the palomino. "And it's a kind of devil's choice." His lips drew back in distaste. Blueberry's captors had the only guns, except for the revolvers in her saddlebag. He could wait till they took her from the horse and focused all their concentration on enjoying her, then make a run for the horse and race off with it. But even if he made it, he'd have to come back for them and they'd be ready and waiting. His other choice was to get close enough to jump one of the five, seize his gun, and bring down as many as he could in one furious burst of fire. He'd at least cut down the odds that way, he grunted. "Either way, it'll be damn hard to put theory into practice, lad," he murmured to the horse, slowing as the five men made for a grass-covered, flat circle of land.

"This'll do just fine," the one said, and they dismounted and pulled Blueberry from the saddle.

Canyon swung to the ground and crept on foot to the edge of the trees, the flat circle directly in front of him. They were pulling Blueberry away from her horse, off to the center of the grass. Making a run for the horse might yet be the best of a bad bargain, Canyon mused. To her credit, Blueberry hadn't made a move toward her saddlebag, aware that at least one pair of eyes were always on her. He knew she wanted the two guns there if she could find a way to get to them later.

Unless—and Canyon felt his breath catch—the guns weren't in the saddlebag at all. Maybe she'd lost them, too. He swore silently. What had seemed perhaps the best of two choices was suddenly a blueprint for disaster.

Blueberry's sharp cry of pain brought his eyes back to her. They had flung her to the ground, and two of the others seized her arms while a third began to tear at her clothes. She kicked out furiously and a fourth rushed in to pin her legs down. He managed to hold one of her legs and swung his body over her to hold her still with his weight. Canyon saw him fumbling at the buttons of his Levi's with one hand while Blueberry was held helpless.

"Hurry up, Beezer, we want our chance," one of the men said, a leer in his voice.

"Bastards. Rotten bastards," Canyon heard Blueberry gasp.

The fifth man had dropped to one knee as he looked

on, anticipation flooding his thin, cruel face. But he was damn close to the others, too close, Canyon grimaced. His eyes went to Blueberry's horse. The animal was easier for him to reach, and his eyes fixed on the saddlebag. It became a roulette wheel of leather and stitches as he stared at it. He had gambled with death before, but usually when there was no other choice. He brought his gaze back to the men. They had Blueberry's skirt up and Canyon saw her long, well-fleshed legs spread apart. Now her cries held more panic than fury. The fifth man's back was still to him where he knelt on one knee. Canyon's eyes flicked to the saddlebag and back to the men. They were there, in plain sight, no question about their presence, and he felt his lips press hard.

The old saying from another land swam through his tumbling thoughts: "The devil you know may be better than the one you don't know." He crouched, gathered the strength of powerful thigh and leg muscles, and sprang forward. He was racing full out when he burst from the trees. The man's back was still to him as he crossed the open circle of land. It was one of the two holding Blueberry's arms that looked up and saw his charging figure. But Canyon had reached the fifth man before the other could cry out in alarm. He slammed into the man, sent the figure sprawling face forward while his hand closed around the butt of the gun in his holster and yanked it out. Canyon rolled onto his stomach and came up firing, his first two targets the two men facing him and holding Blueberry's arms. Both flew backward in sprays of red. Canyon swung the gun, firing as he did. The man atop Blueberry screamed in pain as a bullet tore through his stomach as he tried to turn and get his own gun out.

He toppled sideways, but the fourth man had the time to draw. Canyon dived to one side as a hail of bullets plowed into the grass where he'd been. He rolled again, felt another two shots graze his arm, and halted on his stomach as he emptied the six-gun at the fourth man, who tried to reload. The bullets sent him arching backward, the empty gun with the cylinder hanging open sailing into the air. Canyon swung his body in a half-arc to see the fifth man charging at him, a hunting knife in one hand.

O'Grady pressed the trigger and heard the click of the hammer on an empty chamber. He swore silently, flipped onto his back as the charging figure came down on him with the knife. On his back, he managed to get one arm raised, and his hand closed around the man's wrist with the knife less than six inches from his face. He pressed upward, forcing the man's arm back. Canyon twisted, kicked out, and flipped his body sideways, pulling the figure with him. The man landed on his back and Canyon called on the strength of his powerful deltoids, felt the man's arm hold for a fraction of a second and then give way. The knife came down and into the drifter's chest just over the first rib. The man's gargled cough quickly filled with blood.

Canyon rose, pulled away as the figure turned on its side, knees drawn up, blood-filled gasps staining the grass. He turned away and found Blueberry, on her feet, smoothing her skirt down, her blue eyes wide as she stared at him. "My Colt in your saddlebag?" he asked.

"No," she said. "It was tucked into the waistband of my skirt. It fell out when I was thrown. I saw it go under a bush, but I couldn't get to it."

"We'll go back and get it. That's the first thing we'll do. Get your horse," he growled.

She said nothing and retrieved her horse, followed him silently as he traced steps back to the ledge and the trench. She pointed out the bush, some dozen feet back from the edge of the trench, and he found the ivory-gripped Colt and pushed it into his holster. He turned to see Blueberry digging into her saddlebag and he waited, one hand resting on the butt of the Colt. She pulled out the pocket pistol and offered it to him.

He didn't reach out for it as his eyes narrowed at her. "You telling me something?" he asked.

"I guess so." She nodded soberly.

"You going to start telling me the truth, also?"

"I did!" Blueberry half-pouted. "You just won't believe me."

"You've been selective. I want more."

Blueberry swung to the ground and stared into the distance for a long moment. When she turned back to Canyon, her face was grave. "You still taking me back?"

"I am," Canyon said, and dismounted to stand before her.

"I don't understand it. I don't understand you, Canyon O'Grady. You save me, risk getting yourself killed, all to bring me back to Jake Sanderson?" Blueberry said with exasperation in her voice.

"That's only part of it," Canyon said. "I couldn't leave the likes of you to those scroungers. That would've been a sin."

Little lights came into Blueberry's eyes and she reached up, her mouth touching his, a fleeting kiss, then again, longer this time. "Thank you, Canyon O'Grady." She pulled away. "Maybe we ought to start over."

"Good idea."

"But not here," Blueberry said, and Canyon nodded in understanding.

He climbed back on the palomino and began to lead the way downhill. Blueberry came to ride alongside him as he left the hard, ridged land and made his way to where the hills were longer and the slopes thicker with forest.

She pulled up when they came to a stand of slippery elm where the dense foliage held back the burning sun. "Can we rest? I didn't get much sleep last night," she said.

"Me neither." Canyon smiled and her shrug held unsaid apology. He pushed another few yards deeper under the low branches, halted, and as he swung to the ground, he felt the weariness push at his own body. He stretched out on a bed of bristle grass, which, despite its name, offered a soft cushion. Blueberry lay down alongside him and he watched her fall asleep before he closed his eyes and gave way to tiredness.

When he woke, the sun had moved across the sky. He pushed to his feet, turned, and watched Blueberry rub sleep from her eyes. She shook her head to help herself come awake, and the peach-blond hair sent out shards of yellow.

"Time to talk," he said, and she nodded and pushed to her feet with a graceful motion, her full breasts swaying in unison.

"You've been selective with the truth, too, you know," she said with a half-pout.

"Maybe," he allowed. "But that's not important now. Tell me about Jake Sanderson."

"I'm not his wife or his girlfriend."

"You going to stick to that, are you?"

"I knew you wouldn't believe me," Blueberry snapped. "There's no point in talking to you."

Canyon's eyes peered hard at her and he gave voice to the thoughts that pulled at him. "Maybe you are telling me the truth." He saw the flare of temper leave her bright-blue eyes. "Then why'd he send me after you?"

"I don't know that."

Canyon nodded, accepted the answer. She seemed as honestly perplexed by the question as he. "Tell me more about yourself and Jake Sanderson," he said.

"I worked for him for two months," she said. "Sorting stock, keeping books, odd jobs."

"How'd you come all the way out to Sanderson's operation to find work?" Canyon asked.

"I didn't. I came out here to visit my cousin, Billy Hill. He was always my favorite cousin and the youngest one. He wrote me he had a job with Sanderson's operation. I was dancing in a saloon only a few hundred miles south. I wanted to quit anyway, and coming to see Billy was a good excuse. When I got here, Sanderson offered me the job and I took it," Blueberry explained.

"What do you know about the silver shipments and the raids on them?"

"I used to watch them leave and I heard about the raids. Hill bandits, Sanderson said."

"Seems they're always at the right place at the right time."

"Meaning they knew where to be and when," she said. "Somebody from inside is working with them."

"Seems so to me. You hear about anything like that when you worked for Sanderson?"

"No."

Canyon searched his mind for easy words, phrases that wouldn't bring on her fury, and found none. But he still tried to slide into it. "That still leaves too many questions that don't seem to fit right. You're at the center of most of them, Blueberry," he remarked calmly, and saw her eyes darken instantly.

"What's that supposed to mean?" She frowned.

"You told that trapper you were up here looking for wagon tracks. You asked him if he'd seen any," Canyon reminded her.

"And you think I'm the one passing on the information?" Blueberry exploded.

"I didn't say that. I said there are questions and you keep on being in the middle of them."

"Damn you, Canyon, I thought we were starting over. I thought that meant trusting me," she accused.

"I've got to do more than trust, Blueberry. I've got to know."

"Why? Who are you?" Blueberry threw back.

"Why are you looking for wagon tracks in these hills, Blueberry?" he repeated, ignoring her question.

"Because I'm looking for Billy," she shot back.

Canyon waited, saw her fight down anger, and her eyes suddenly filled with tears she shook away. "Go on," he said, and she drew her breath in, her breasts pressing the shirt smooth.

"Billy was one of the crew that took the last shipment out," Blueberry said. "It was raided, as most of the others, but they made it through to the storage depot. But Billy never came back."

"Sanderson changed crews at the end of every trip, he said," Canyon reminded her.

"Yes, I know."

"So Billy wouldn't be coming back to go out again," Canyon said. "Maybe he and the others went off on another job. Or maybe he stayed on to enjoy himself with the others. They'd been paid off."

"I know, maybe, maybe. But it's not like Billy to do that."

"You sure of that?" Canyon asked, not ungently.

Blueberry's full lips pressed hard into each other. "No, I'm not sure. I hadn't seen Billy for over a year before I came here to visit him."

"Young men change, grow up," Canyon said.

She shrugged unhappily. "Maybe, but none of the others ever came back either."

"They wouldn't. Sanderson was going to use a new crew for the next shipment. They were through," Canyon reminded her again.

Blueberry looked away, her silence sending out waves of unhappiness. She turned her eyes back to him after a moment. "I know, but I still have a bad feeling about it. That's why I want to keep looking."

"You should never have come up here alone in the first place. You're lucky you're not in some Pawnee tepee by now," Canyon said. "You're going back with me. You say you don't know why Jake Sanderson sent me after you. I surely don't either. We'll find the answer together." He watched her nod, step to him, and put her head against his chest. The shadows of twilight had begun to slide down the hills. "This is as good a place as any to bed down," Canyon said. "We'll make the depot tomorrow."

She stepped back, her face somber, and helped him unsaddle the horses. He made a small fire afterward as night came, and she finished the last can of her beef and beans over the flames. When the meal was finished, he took out his bedroll and stretched out on it as Blueberry folded herself down along one edge, her eyes searching his face.

"Why do you have to do more than trust?" she asked. "Why do you have to know? Who are you, O'Grady?"

"I told you."

"You told me a fairy tale."

"Fairy tales begin with once upon a time." Canyon laughed.

"Some begin with I was sent as a scout and extra gun."

"Maybe, when I've all my answers, we can talk more."

"That's all?" she pressed.

"For now," he said, and she drew a large sigh.

"Then you'll be only one thing for me now: the person who risked his life for me. That's pretty damn wonderful. Nobody's ever done that," Blueberry said.

"My pleasure," Canyon said. The moon was trickling down through the leaves to join the soft glow of the firelight. "It's time to get some sleep," he suggested. He sat up and began to unbutton his shirt. Blueberry rose to her feet, went to the saddlebag, and took out a nightdress. She stepped behind a tree, and when she reappeared, Canyon had undressed to his underwear bottoms. She came to him and he saw her eyes move across the breadth of his shoulders and the smoothly muscled contours of his chest. A light-gray nightdress with a square neck, tied with a drawstring, hung almost to the ground as it clung to the fullness of her breasts.

"I don't know why I put this on," Blueberry said. "Seeing as how I don't intend to keep it on."

"A sense of propriety is like a limpet on a rock. It's very hard to shake loose," Canyon said.

Blueberry dropped to her knees beside him, reached one hand up, and pulled at the tiny drawstring at the neck of the nightdress; the garment fell open. Her breasts spilled forward, and with a shake of her shoulders the nightdress fell away entirely and she let his eyes take in her loveliness. "It's not just saying thank you, though I suppose there's a little of that in it," she murmured. "It's also desire. I've felt that since the first moment we met."

"Good. I like that better."

"You send out waves, Canyon O'Grady. You're a charmer even when you're being rotten."

"And you're a handsome lass, Blueberry Hill," he said as he took in her broad shoulders, collarbone prominent above the slow curve of her breasts. His gaze lingered on the way their full cups curved up, each centered with a dark-red tip on a light-red circle. She had a broad rib cage that quickly narrowed to a small waist, a flat abdomen beneath it, and then a little belly that held a delicious little curve to it. Her thighs were full yet slender, knees rounded, and her calves a long, graceful line. She leaned toward him and her breasts swayed together, not unlike peaches on a tree, and he reached out and cupped both in his hands.

Blueberry gave a tiny shudder of delight and he drew her against him as he lay back and felt the wonderful warm softness of her against his skin, the little dark-red tips pressing into his chest, already growing firm. He turned on his side with her as he pushed away the last of his clothing and felt his own surging desire, flesh growing strong, throbbing, seeking. He pressed his mouth on hers and Blueberry's lips parted at once for him, answering his kisses hungrily, her tongue a slipping, sliding little messenger.

His hand caressed her breast and she shuddered again with delight as he let his thumb move slowly back and forth over the dark-red nipple. "Oh, oh, yes, nice . . . nice," Blueberry breathed, and her arms wrapped tightly around his neck. When his lips moved down along the side of her neck, she uttered a soft moan. When he found her breast and closed around the softness of her, pulling gently, caressing, resting his lips on the very tip, the soft moan became a half-gasped cry. Her hands came up to push through his flame-red hair as she pressed her breasts up for his mouth. "Yes, yes, ooooh, oh, yes," Blueberry groaned, and he felt her body half-turn, lift, and then fall back again.

He let his hand move slowly, tantalizingly down her rib cage, across the flat abdomen, tracing an imaginary line along the convex curve of her belly. Her body began to quiver. When he pushed into the tangly dense black V, Blueberry's hands dug into his back and small gasping sounds fell from her lips. He pressed down farther, reached the bottom of the tangly triangle, and touched the softness where her thighs met. "Oh, oh, God . . . oh," Blueberry cried out, words only the echo of the flesh, all the senses gathered in anticipation. He touched deeper, came to the luscious portal, and Blueberry gave a sharp half-scream as she quivered and her thighs fell apart, then came together again around his hand, which reached deeper.

"Yes, yes . . . oh, yes . . . oh, oh," Blueberry gasped, and again her thighs fell open as his hand touched the wet softness. She groaned in pleasure. He felt his own pulsating desire pushing at him and he brought his legs over hers and rested the warmth of his throbbing eagerness against the tangly black triangle.

"Oh, oh, God," Blueberry cried out. Her torso rose, thrusting upward while her legs lifted to come against his hips. "Please, please, oh, yes, please," she gasped out.

Canyon let himself slide from her pubic mount and find the moist heat of her. Her breathy cries became a half-scream as he slid forward, filling her softness, throbbing against the sweet cage. Blueberry moved with him, pushing herself forward with his every sliding thrust, drawing back, then ramming forward again, and each time a tiny cry of pure delight came from her, a rhythmic litany of joy that grew louder and hoarser as he thrust harder, the rhythm changing, desire taking hold of deliberateness, the command of the senses, beyond denying, beyond questioning.

Blueberry's body began to quiver again; he saw her eyes grow wide, her lips fall open. "Canyon . . . oh, Canyon . . . now, now, oh, now," she breathed, and pulled his face to hers, her lips devouring, her tongue a hot, lashing, seeking probe. He felt her warm softness tightening around him in contractions of ecstasy. Her cries began to rise, the small gasps growing louder, higher in pitch until, with an explosion of sound, Blueberry screamed in pure and total rapture, all the violent spasms of ecstasy exploding, breaking loose to carry him along with her, and he heard his own groaned cry of gratification.

Blueberry's full breasts shook against his chest and her scream finally died away to tiny wimpered sounds as her quivering began to grow less. But her thighs stayed closed hard around him, the flesh trying to cling to pleasure, unwilling to accept the transience of ecstasy until finally, with a sigh of despair, Blueberry lay back on the bedroll and her legs dropped away from him in a reluctant gesture of finality. "Damn," he heard her murmur, and he smiled.

"Maybe it wouldn't be as good if it were longer," he said.

"I'd like to try," she grumbled, and pressed herself hard against him. She snuggled herself comfortably into almost instant sleep, his hand resting against the peach-blond hair.

Maybe there was nothing more to Blueberry Hill than the explanations she had given him. Canyon wanted to believe that. He wanted to believe her. But believing was a luxury he couldn't afford. There were still too many questions. He'd let enjoyment and pleasure take the place of believing for now. Tomorrow was only a few hours away.

He closed his eyes and let himself enjoy the warmth of her against him as he slept.

5

When morning came, Canyon enjoyed watching Blueberry lazily stir to wakefulness, wash with water from her canteen, and finally pull on her clothes, every motion a graceful ballet of movement, simple and guileless and made of completely natural beauty. " 'If eyes were made for seeing, then Beauty is its own excuse for being,' " Canyon said. "Emerson wrote that, and he was so right."

She came to him and held him against the softness of her breasts for a moment. "So many scouts and gunhands quote poetry," she murmured.

"A taste for it, nurtured by the good friars when I was a lad. It's never left me," he told her. He pushed to his feet and took her with him. "But we have to leave here," he said, and quickly saddled the horses.

When he led the way down the hills, Blueberry rode beside him and again he smiled at her instinctive acuity as she caught the tiny furrows that came to his brow.

"What is it?" she asked, and he pointed to the marks of unshod ponies.

"Indian ponies," he told her. "All over these hills. This is their land. Pawnee, probably." He turned the palomino and led the way into tree cover. "We'll stay away from open places as much as we can. It'll add a few hours to the trip but we're more likely to have our scalps on when we get there.''

Blueberry rode in silence beside him. Staying in tree cover added more than a few hours; it was late afternoon when Canyon rode out of the base of the hills onto flatland and turned north. He shot a long glance at Blueberry as the depot came into sight, but her pretty face showed only unconcerned calmness.

Canyon's gaze swept the depot as he rode in with her, and he quickly saw that the eight Owensboro mountain wagons he'd seen on his first visit were now only four. The handful of troopers were doing their tasks by the small barracks. He reined to a halt in front of Jake Sanderson's office, dismounted, and knocked on the door. No one answered, so he knocked again, with the same results. He saw a blue uniform with sergeant's stripes coming toward him.

The trooper halted, a square-jawed man with a day's stubble on his face. "You looking for Jake Sanderson?" the sergeant asked.

"I am," Canyon answered.

"He's not here. He took the last shipment out," the soldier said.

Canyon saw Blueberry swing from her horse, a faint arch to her eyebrows.

"The last shipment was canceled." Canyon frowned.

"I wouldn't know anything about that, sir," the sergeant said. "But a shipment came in and Sanderson took it out with a new crew."

"When?" Canyon barked.

"Two days ago," the sergeant said.

"Much obliged, Sergeant," Canyon said as he turned to Blueberry and met the amused smile on her lips.

"Now you know why Jake Sanderson sent you after

me with that wild story about my being his wife,"
Blueberry said. "He sent you on a wild-goose chase."
She gave him a long, sideways glance. "Don't tell me
you're not thinking the same thing."

"The thought came to me," Canyon admitted. "But
I could be doing the man a disservice. The shipment
may have come entirely unexpectedly and he decided
he couldn't wait around for however long it'd take me
to get back with you."

Blueberry tossed back disbelief in her eyes and in
the tolerant smile she offered.

"I'll be finding out," Canyon said. "The sergeant
said it's been only two days. There'll be no trouble
picking up wagon tracks only two days old."

"Then let's get started. We've some daylight left,"
Blueberry said.

"Whoa, now, lass. I'll be going on this alone."

"No you won't. Maybe Sanderson has the answers
to why Billy didn't come back. I'm going to find out,"
she said.

"I'll find out for you. I don't know what I might be
running into on this. I'll not have time for wet-
nursing."

Her eyes flared at once. "You won't have to wet-
nurse me, Canyon O'Grady. I'll take care of myself."

"Maybe and maybe not. I'll not be chancing it on
this. If I'm wrong about Jake Sanderson, it'll be bad.
You stay here. I'm sure there's somewhere you can
stay," Canyon said.

"I'll follow you," Blueberry snapped defiantly. "I
can ride wherever I please."

Canyon's face grew stiff. "Don't do it, Blueberry,
not on this. If you follow me, I'll tie you to the nearest
tree if that's what it takes to keep you from getting
yourself killed." She glowered in silence at him. "I'm
doing what's best for you," he said.

"You're doing what's best for yourself."

"In this case they're one and the same," Canyon said. He reached out to her and she shook him away; he turned and strode toward the barracks. Stubborn and headstrong, she was, but then he'd learned that already. He found the sergeant helping two of his troopers mend a cinch. "Got another question for you, Sergeant. Why hasn't Sanderson taken your men on any of the shipments?"

"I've only half a squad here. My orders are to guard the silver while it's here. It's Sanderson's responsibility to get the silver from here to the storage place, where there's a whole platoon on duty," the sergeant said.

"All right." Canyon nodded. "You've some place a person can stay here?"

"Yes, sir. We keep two rooms beside the barracks for visitors," the soldier said.

"Much obliged. You'll be getting someone for a few days at least," Canyon said, and turned away. He pulled himself onto the palomino and walked the horse to where Blueberry waited, glowering. "Go see the sergeant. He'll show you a place to stay," he said.

"Thank you, kind sir." Her words were coated with mock gratefulness.

"This is good-bye, then, unless you're here when I get back," he said.

"Don't count on it."

"Think about waiting. I'd like that."

"Take me with you. I'd like that," she snapped back.

He blew her a kiss as he put the palomino into a trot and rode from the depot without looking back. There wasn't much day left but he quickly picked up the wagon tracks. Four riders alongside the four wagons, a driver with each wagon, perhaps three guards on the wagons, but he couldn't be certain of that. Eight men, at least, and he saw the wagon tracks led north for another mile before turning up into the Flint Hills, where a wide passage beckoned.

He followed till darkness came, and he bedded down, still in the base of the hills, under a low-branched box elder. He lay down on his bedroll and thoughts tumbled through his mind, most about Jake Sanderson. If Blueberry were right, if the man had concocted the entire story about her to send him on a wild-goose chase, that would make him the key to everything.

The possibility seemed to grow stronger almost by the minute. Sanderson was certainly in a position to plan it all. He could even have planned the ambush little Amy Dillard overheard. Washington had sent Sanderson word they were sending an extra gunhand and scout, Canyon mused. Yet there were still things that didn't fit right, things that failed to make sense, and he pushed away further speculation. He'd not let himself jump the wrong way. He'd have the truth of it in a few days, he reminded himself, and he closed his eyes and let sleep sweep over him.

When morning came, he concentrated on following the wheel tracks again, the marks still clear and easy to see. The passage grew narrower, turned up, and then became a series of rises and hollows. The wagons were now moving along behind one another. He had followed the tracks up a rise and just started down the dip on the other side when he saw the wagon blocking the passage, a one-horse farm wagon with low sides. The right front wheel had come off and lay along-side the wagon; a man was trying unsuccessfully to bring the wheel in place. Canyon noted the figure lying in the back of the wagon, covered with a blanket, a bonnet sitting on top of long brown hair.

The man saw him and began to wave frantically at him as Canyon swore under his breath. He had no time for good deeds and no stomach for turning his back on somebody that needed help. He rode forward toward the wagon as the man continued to beckon him.

"Just help me get the wheel on, mister," the man said. "My wife's awful sick with the fever. I was tryin' to get her to the doctor when this damn wheel came off." Canyon allowed a deep sigh as he swung from the palomino. A conscience was the price of a good upbringing, he muttered. "Been trying to get this wheel on for an hour. I can't do it alone," the man said.

Canyon had just gone past the wagon with the blanketed and bonneted figure inside it when he heard the sound, turned, and saw the woman sitting up. Her bonnet fell off as she did, and O'Grady saw the big, heavy Joslyn Army revolver in her hand, only she had become a thick-lipped, big-nosed man wearing an ill-fitting brown wig.

"Surprise, dead man." The figure laughed, and Canyon saw the man's finger tighten on the trigger. He flung himself sideways in a twisting, spinning dive, but the gun went off, the range almost point-blank. The lower part of his back seemed to explode in pain as he hit the ground and shafts of fire raced up his spine.

Suddenly he could see nothing, hear nothing, and feel nothing. He lay as if in a void of blackness; he knew he was trying to move his limbs, but he was totally devoid of feeling. Yet he was not dead—not yet, anyway. He clung to a kind of suspended awareness, as though he were detached from himself. Perhaps this was the first stage of dying, he wondered, the spirit freed to hang alone in a halfway world, no longer tied to feeling, hearing, seeing.

Yet the strange, suspended awareness persisted. Was it supposed to be this way? Were there questions after death? If anything else was happening to him, he didn't know of it. The soundless, timeless void stayed, a cocoon of nothingness, and then, slowly, like a tattered scarf fraying away, the suspended awareness began to drift away and finally there was not even that. He lay in nothingness, the world not even a memory.

Cold. He suddenly felt coldness. He had no way of knowing why, but the awareness had returned. The coldness of death? No, he answered himself. The dead didn't feel. Or did they? What do the living know? But he felt coldness, deep down someplace, unfocused at first, then finding focus. It was at the base of his spine, and it felt good. The void was still with him but it had been pierced. He could feel, and that was more than awareness. Something else stirred deep inside him, an excitement, and that too was piercing the void. The coldness came to him again, soothing, and suddenly the timeless void began to roll away. He could feel more than the coldness. He could feel his eyelids moving, thoughts no longer suspended awareness but concrete perceptions. He lived. No matter what else. He lived and felt the spiral of excitement surging inside him.

His eyelids moved again and he exercised willpower and felt them come open. He blinked and it was still darkness. But the darkness was different. Soft, real, a faint warm wind, not the timeless void beyond unconsciousness. The coldness at the base of his spine had stopped now and he tried his body, felt the reality of it, his fingers move, curl, straighten out. He blinked again and his eyes focused, saw a blanket, and he pressed down on his hands, almost cried out in triumph as his body lifted. But the strength disappeared and he fell back to the blanket, felt the softness of it, and he forced strength through his arms again. He started to turn and felt himself being assisted; he pushed himself onto one elbow and blinked away a momentary veil that crossed his eyes.

A shape swam into sight, took on definition, and became peach-blond hair and a round face. He heard the gasped sound of his own breath. His lips moved, tried to form words, but his throat was dry and the face moved away to return with a canteen to hold to his lips.

He drank eagerly, finally stopped and pushed himself higher onto his elbow to stare at Blueberry. "I thought I was dead," Canyon murmured.

"They thought so, too," Blueberry said, and with an almost angry rush the images raced through his mind, the man calling for help, the woman in the wagon, the woman becoming a pistol-carrying figure, the blast of the gun as he tried to dive away.

"You found me?" Canyon asked.

"I came up at the end of it. There was nothing I could do but follow. I thought they'd killed you."

"Follow where?"

"They didn't leave you there. They threw you in the wagon and drove another half-mile into the trees and tossed you out, then drove away," she said. "I waited till I was sure they were gone and ran to you."

He frowned at her. The warm wind blew and he felt it against his skin, and he frowned again and looked down at himself. He was naked, he saw. "You seemed dead, yet you were still breathing. They plainly thought you'd stop that soon enough," Blueberry said. "The bullet apparently grazed the base of your spine and cut off all feeling as well as everything else. In a way you were lucky. If you hadn't seemed all but dead, they'd have finished the job."

"How did you know I wasn't going to be dead in a few minutes?" Canyon asked her.

"I didn't, but I didn't see any blood on you, so I pulled your clothes off and found the place at the bottom of your spine. The bullet had gone through the flesh but apparently touched a collection of nerve endings. To be honest, I didn't know exactly what to do, so I started applying cold compresses to the spot."

"How long?" Canyon asked.

"Since this morning and through most of tonight," she said. "Almost twenty-four hours. It'll be dawn soon."

"Cormac, what'd they do with Cormac?" Canyon asked in sudden alarm.

"Nothing. I retrieved him. He's with my horse in the trees," Blueberry answered. "But I don't think you'll be riding any."

"We'll see. I've got to ride. I've got to keep after Sanderson."

"Duty first, Agent O'Grady?" she asked with her brows arched, a smug smile edging her lips. "I went through your things, found the card at the bottom of your saddlebag." He blew a deep sigh at her and the smug smile remained. "Aren't you glad I didn't pay attention to you and stay at the depot?" she slid at him.

He found a smile and knew there was ruefulness in it. "I guess I am," he murmured. "And if I'm not, I should be."

"Try to move some more," she said, and leaned back.

"Like putting some clothes on? I feel naked as a jaybird," he said.

"You are, and I like it this way," Blueberry said. "Just move about some."

He pushed up on both elbows and felt the sharp stab

of pain at the base of his spine. He half-turned and the pain came again, but it was bearable. He drew his knees up and it grew no worse. She offered a hand for him to stand, but he declined it and pulled on his thigh muscles. The pain came again at once but still bearable, and he rose to his feet, took a few steps, lengthened his stride, and returned to stand before Blueberry. The pain remained yet no worse now than pains he'd had before and he met her eyes.

"I ought to be able to thank you properly by tomorrow night," he said.

"You better," she answered smugly, and folded herself down beside him as he lay down again on the blanket. She rubbed her hands over his body, a soothing, firm, yet gentle massage, and he watched her plainly enjoy the doing of it. "No more talk about my staying behind, I trust," she said as she pressed a hand over his muscled chest.

"No more, but I'd still like it better if you would," he told her.

"You're not giving Jake Sanderson the benefit of the doubt any longer, I take it," she said, and he felt his mouth tighten.

"No, not after those two bushwhackers. They were planted there, waiting for me. Sanderson knew if I came back early I'd follow these wagon tracks up into the base of the hills. All he had to do was have those two waiting there," Canyon said, bitterness in his voice. "That puts him in the middle of it."

"You think Sanderson's the one who's been passing on the information about the shipments to the raiders?" Blueberry asked.

"I'm thinking he's a lot more than that. I'm thinking he's the key to all of it, the man that's put the whole thing together. If I'm right, he's done a lot of clever things."

"Such as?"

"Changing crews for every shipment. If he kept the same crew, somebody might have seen something, heard something, or just gotten suspicious," Canyon said. "Changing crews each shipment prevented that. But even more important, it made him look both efficient and innocent, just a man trying everything he could to stop the raids."

"When all the while he was planning the details of each and every one," Blueberry said.

Canyon nodded even as he found himself frowning into space. The same questions rose up to hang in his mind again. "Something still doesn't add up," he muttered. "Why have the raiders taken only a few boxes or a single chest? Why not make off with a whole damn shipment? That still doesn't fit right."

Blueberry shrugged helplessly.

"I'm missing something here," Canyon said. "I can't figure what, but something." He drew a deep breath and lay back. "And I'm suddenly tired."

Blueberry quickly shed clothes and folded her smooth-skinned nakedness against him. Tiredness swept over him with a rush and forced his eyes to close as she lay with her peach-blond hair into the curve of his shoulder and one leg half across his thighs. He began to quickly drift into slumber, aware that he was both lucky and grateful. The way of the Good Samaritan is still hard, he murmured to himself as he fell asleep.

The sun was high across the hills when he woke and Blueberry slid from him. She sat up and rubbed sleep from her eyes as he took in the loveliness of her full-cupped breasts, which moved in unison. He dressed slowly and carefully. The pain was still there, though not so sharp.

"I don't think you should ride yet," Blueberry said as she watched him.

"Got to. We've lost too much time already," Canyon said, but he took his blanket, folded it carefully, and laid it across the back of the saddle where the seat and the cantle came together. It made an almost perfect cushion and he was grateful for it being there as he climbed onto the palomino and began to ride. He led the way back to the wagon tracks and turned upward after them as they curved into the hills. It wasn't till late afternoon that he put the palomino into a trot and rode without too much pain. The wagon tracks seemed almost to wander through the hills, but he realized that Sanderson was following whatever opened up as the smoothest path, mostly old moose and deer trails.

A gray filter began to spread over the sun before the day ended. Canyon paused to scan the sky. "We could be getting rain by morning," he said.

"That ought to slow wagons down," Blueberry commented.

"It might," Canyon said. "I want to reach them before they're raided again."

He cast another glance at the sky and held the palomino in a trot until darkness descended. A small arbor between red maples offered a good place to stop for the night, and when he swung to the ground, he felt the exhaustion come over him, his back a strained, throbbing muscle.

Blueberry shared his pemmican with him, downing the meal with an effort.

"It takes getting used to, lass," he said, and the meal finished, he took down his bedroll and undressed. He lay back and the exhaustion demanded sleep as Blueberry folded herself against him. He drew the top of the bedroll over their bodies as the warm night wind turned damp and they quickly slept.

The new day came and he woke to a mud-gray sky, a handful of raindrops flung against his face by the wind. Blueberry stirred herself as he woke her; she made a face at the sky and quickly pulled on her clothes. After he found a clump of blackberries that served as breakfast, he donned a rain slicker and handed Blueberry an extra one. He set off after the wagon tracks again as the rain changed from a few sprinkles to a heavy, wind-driven downpour. Blueberry became a shrouded shape sometimes hardly visible. He had to squint through the downpour at the wagon tracks that continued to move up into the hills.

By midday, Canyon felt the palomino slipping as the ground grew soft. He halted when the rain lightened for a few minutes. He swept the hills and grimaced. Too high, too steep-sided, quickly growing too soft, he muttered. He scanned the hills again, as much as he could see before the rain began to drive down on him once more, pushed by a wind that rolled down from the higher hills. But he thought he had glimpsed a side of stone and he pulled alongside Blueberry's hunched and shrouded figure.

She peered at him through the sheets of rain as he pointed to a path that led to the right. "What about the tracks?" she asked.

"We'll pick them up tomorrow."

"This rain could wash them away."

He nodded grimly, her words an echo of the thoughts that had already passed through his mind. "It damn well could," he agreed. "But we won't pick them up if we're buried under a ton of mud." He motioned for her to follow and turned the palomino onto the narrow path. The usually surefooted horse wavered under him as the ground slid beneath his feet and Canyon let the animal pick his own way upward.

O'Grady wiped his eyes clear of the rain for an instant, enough to get his bearings and catch another glimpse of the rock. It seemed farther away than it had the first time, and he swore softly and glanced across at Blueberry. Her horse had fallen back and was plainly having a harder time than Cormac in maintaining its footing. "Give me the reins," he called to her, and she tossed the straps to him. He held the reins taut as the palomino fought upward, but he quickly tossed them back to Blueberry: his horse couldn't dig in firmly enough to pull the other steed along. He bent his head down as a blast of wind drove the rain at him as though a giant bucket had been flung in his face.

Blueberry was a good length behind him now, he saw as he glanced back. But he couldn't afford to slow down, and once again he halted, wiped his eyes clear, and swept the hills. He felt his lips turn down. The grayness remained unbroken, the sky still pouring rain down in driving sheets. Alarm grew inside him as he saw narrow strips of topsoil sliding down the hillsides. The strips could become wider ones and, in a flash, turn into a cascade of sliding, rain-soaked earth. He had to find a cave or a protected ledge before that happened.

He continued to drive the palomino toward the tall side of stone, but the narrow path suddenly vanished. He halted to see Blueberry at least two lengths back. He waved at her until she saw him and waved back and turned her horse to follow him. He rode across the center of the hill and felt the palomino slide and slip as he crossed the hillside.

The wall of rock rose up closer now, a rainswept wall that began to take on definition. He saw the uneven surface of it and then a series of protrusions on the face of it, small ledges all too shallow to afford shelter. But the rock rose up along the edge of the hill and Canyon turned the palomino upward alongside the sweeping expanse of stone. When the palomino halted to rest legs grown tired from fighting uphill on the soft, slipping, clutching earth, Canyon waited for Blueberry to catch up to him again. As she neared, he could hear the harsh snorting of her horse above the sound of the rain, and he took his lasso from the fork swell and tossed one end to her.

"Tie it around yourself," he said, and watched while she made two loops around her waist with the rope and tied it securely; he looped his end of the lariat around his arm and sent the palomino forward again. He let the lariat stay slack as Blueberry quickly fell behind again, the rope a precaution and a hope and nothing more. He had already learned the palomino couldn't pull her horse along on the slippery footing.

Now Canyon peered hard along the base of the stone wall as he slowly moved up alongside it. "A cave, dammit," he swore into the wind and the rain. "Where are the damn caves?" A rock formation such as the high stone rise usually held at least two, sometimes three caves, he knew. His eyes strained through the rain, searching for a darker, deeper tone against the unremitting grayness. He had climbed perhaps another hundred yards—and taken almost an hour to do so—the rope around his arm slack, Blueberry at least four lengths down the hill from him, when he heard the gasp of excitement escape his rain-covered lips.

A dark and arched patch appeared another dozen yards on in the stone wall. He urged the palomino forward, pulled to his right to move to the very edge of the wall. The rope on his arm tightened for a moment and he allowed another length of line out as he reached the edge of the stone. A narrow line of earth retained more firmness, and the palomino pulled itself gratefully along the more solid section. The dark place in the stone became an opening, tall enough to let the horse in, and Canyon allowed himself a smile just as he reached the cave entrance. He started in with the palomino, ducked his head low to barely clear the top. The cave was set back in the rock—dry, deep enough, and with enough air to hold only a faint muskiness.

Canyon started to dismount when the sound came to him, the sucking, oozing sound first, and a curse fell from his lips as Blueberry's scream split the air. The rope around his arm sprang into a taut, snapping spring. He felt himself go down onto his knees, dragged toward the entrance of the cave. He managed to reach out to a flat slab of rock that protruded from the inside wall. He caught at it, slipped, and caught at it again just long enough to wrap a length of the lariat around it. Blueberry's screams still pierced the air, rising over the deep, sliding sound of tons of mud slithering down the hillside.

Canyon pulled to his feet, looped another three turns of the lariat around the rock protrusion, and ran for the mouth of the cave. Holding on to the rope with one hand, he plunged into the rain and his feet were immediately swept out from under him by the mud slide. He let himself go, but clung to the rope with both hands as the mud swept him down.

A half-gargled scream drifted to him, then silence. He cursed as the mud clutched at his legs. He tightened his grip on the rope and brought himself to a halt to let his eyes sweep the hillside of gray mud that continued to slide downward. Blueberry had stopped screaming, and he took one hand from the rope to wipe the rain from his eyes. He scanned the hill again, followed the line of the rope, and saw the small bulge sliding down with the mud. Clinging to the rope, he let the mud push him downward with surprising speed and he reached the bulge where the rope disappeared into the mud. Cursing, he clawed at the mud, which slid back almost as fast as he threw it up with both hands. He braced his legs and felt the mud quickly build up against his back, pressing harder with each passing moment.

Suddenly his hands touched cloth and he clawed with furious desperation. He grasped an arm, pulled, and Blueberry came out from the mud, a gray shape coated with the ooze. He pulled again as the mud against his back grew so heavy he had difficulty breathing. Getting one arm around the mud-coated form, he twisted his body and the ooze at his back slid past. He clung to the rope and Blueberry's face emerged as the rain quickly washed away the coating of mud that covered her.

She had her lips tightly closed, Canyon saw, and he bent his face down to hers. With relief, he felt the soft touch of breath that escaped her lips. She was unconscious but alive, and using every muscle in his shoulders and back, he began to pull himself along the rope with one hand. The sliding mud clung to his legs and feet like a giant, fingerless hand that tried to drag him backward. He inched his way up, Blueberry a limp weight in one arm. He had to halt often, and each time the ooze pulled at him with renewed strength. He began to lose feeling in his right arm where he held Blueberry as his muscles began to cramp. With an oath flung into the rain, he began to pull himself upward again, and his hand began to feel as though it were being cut in two.

O'Grady felt the strength ebbing from him, but now the rain had become an unexpected ally as it helped to keep the mud from congealing around his legs. Each second seemed a minute and each minute an hour. With bitter despair rising inside him, he realized he had little strength left. Drawing a deep breath, he pulled upward again, halted, closed his eyes, and blinked them open again. The dark, arched area came into sight, and with a cry of desperate renewal, he drew on a wellspring of strength from deep within his aching body. He fastened his eyes on the dark area as a drowning man pursues a life preserver, and he began to pull upward once more. The darkened area grew larger, became the mouth of the cave, and he fought away the searing pain that consumed him. The rain continued to drive down and the mud kept pulling at his legs as it slid downward. It seemed that all the world was sliding away in a gray ooze.

But the mouth of the cave was there, only a dozen feet away now, and he half-laughed and half-cursed as he pulled the last, searing, aching distance to fall onto the firmness of the rock flooring at the edge of the cave. He dragged Blueberry up with him and lay there, his every breath a hoarse, wheezing, strangled sound. He lay still and let a measure of strength return to his body. He lifted his head only when he heard the soft groan from beside him.

Blueberry groaned again and her eyelids flickered, then finally came open as Canyon pushed himself to a sitting position. Her eyes slowly focused on him, the shock and horror still gripping her face, and she raised on one elbow and fell against him, her head buried in his chest.

"My God, I thought I was dead, I surely did," she breathed. "It came, knocked the horse down, and I was thrown free. But then it just swept over me. It was horrible. All I could think of was not to swallow any of it, so I kept my mouth closed."

"That's probably why you're alive now," Canyon told her.

"But it just poured all over me, covered me, and it was heavy, a terrible weight. I blacked out," Blueberry said. She pushed herself tighter against him.

He held her, lifted his hands to examine the deep creases that were dug into his left palm. Somehow, for all the creases, pain and deepness, the hand hadn't bled and he was grateful for small favors. A damp wind blew into the cave and Blueberry shivered. He looked down at her mud-caked clothes. The daylight, though gray, afforded enough light for him to see that there was an assortment of dry pieces of wood inside the cave, some kindling size, others larger, and all of it no doubt brought in by animals over the years.

"We need a fire," he said, and detached himself from her. He gathered the small kindling pieces, some so dry they were almost straw, and had a fire burning quickly enough. He added two of the larger pieces of wood until the entire cave was lighted and warm. He pulled Blueberry to her feet and, his arm around her waist, began to walk her toward the mouth of the cave. She shrank back instantly. "It's all right. There's a small edge of solid rock just beyond the entrance," he said.

"What are we going to do?" Blueberry asked, fear still in her voice.

"Stand there and let the rain wash all the mud from our clothes first," he said.

"And then?"

"Undress, let the rain wash us down, and then lay our clothes by the fire. They'll have all night to dry," he said.

She held his hand as he carefully stepped onto the rock ledge that extended not more than six inches beyond the mouth of the cave. He let the rain wash the mud from their clothes, stepped back, and began to undress. Blueberry pulled off her clothes and stood close beside him as he stepped, naked, onto the ledge again. The rain poured down over them and he turned with her as though they were standing under a shower.

"I'm cold," she said, shivering, after a few minutes.

He hurried her back into the cave, where the warmth of the fire surrounded them at once. He lay their clothes alongside one wall already warmed by the fire and then went to the palomino, took down his bedroll and an extra blanket, and spread the coverings on the stone.

Blueberry folded herself down beside him and held tight against him while outside the rain continued to drench the land and the mud still slithered down the hillside. He lay still and let his pulled and aching muscles relax in the healing warmth of the fire. He dozed, woke, and dozed again, Blueberry beside him.

He woke again when the day turned into night and he heard the rain outside begin to lessen. He felt better, the fire's warmth penetrating. Blueberry ate some of the pemmican with him before lying down again at his side.

"What happens tomorrow?" she asked.

"If the rain stops soon, we wait and see how quickly the morning sun dries out the ground," he said. "Good hot sun can dry things out with surprising speed. We might be able to ride before noon."

"My horse has been killed, I guess."

"Maybe. Can't be sure. A big, heavy animal can just as easily be carried downhill and survive instead of being covered over quickly as you were," Canyon said.

"What about Sanderson and the wagons? They'd have no chance against a mud slide like this."

"Maybe it didn't hit them. They were a day ahead of us. They could've been near forest land, where they could ride it out protected," Canyon said. "But they will be slowed tomorrow. They'll have to wait longer for the ground to become firm enough to support wagons heavy with silver. Maybe we can close some distance tomorrow."

Blueberry nodded as he rose and put one of the last of the larger pieces of wood onto the fire. He paused to admire her naked loveliness before settling down beside her again, her skin with a faint orange blush to it in the firelight, the peach-blond hair glistening. But his muscles ached and he lay still beside her, muttering silently about the price of heroism. Blueberry lay against him, one arm across his chest as sleep swept across him. He closed his eyes, his exhaustion not to be denied.

He slept heavily, the cave silent and snug and his body restoring itself in the fire's warmth. It was the hanging hour just before dawn when he woke, his eyes still half-closed, a pleasant sensation on his skin. He stayed unmoving a minute longer, more aware of the sensation, warm and more than pleasant, he decided. He felt softness moving across his abdomen, down over his flat, muscled belly, and then an extra warmth cupping his groin, touching, caressing.

He opened his eyes, looked down to see the peach-blond head half lying on his groin. Blueberry's hand was stroking, caressing. He felt his maleness stirring instantly. He pushed up on one elbow and she felt him move, pressed her head harder into his groin as her fingers clasped around him, soft strokings, fingertips tracing tiny circles around the tip of the burgeoning shaft. She shifted her body and he felt the softness of her lips on him, sweetness of sensation, delicious currents of pleasure.

"Yes, oh, yes," Blueberry murmured, and he heard the delight in her breathy gasps. She pressed harder against him, each motion taking on new delight for her and certainly for him. Suddenly, with a cry of eager urgency, she swung her body around, her legs straddling him, and she thrust herself down onto his rigid, seeking member.

"Oh, ooooooh, yes, oh, oh," Blueberry half-screamed, her head thrown back and her eyes closed. Her lovely full-cupped breast swayed from side to side as she thrust down again and again, pushing hard with her knees as if she couldn't fill enough of herself with him. He felt his own hips lift to thrust upward, met her every downward, impaling plunge. She screamed in utter delight. The storm of the senses gathered speed, grew wild beyond the control of mere flesh, and suddenly a deep groan rose from Blueberry. It became a wild cry and she fell forward, pressing her breasts into his face. He felt her body begin to quiver. With a last, upward thrust, he let his own sweeping ecstasy explode with her cry that lay somewhere between a groan and a scream.

She stayed atop him, clung, quivered. He felt the sweet claspings around him while rivers of ecstasy traveled through his body. Finally, with a groaning sigh, Blueberry fell atop him and lay still, her breasts wonderfully soft against his face. She stayed atop him until time and flesh insisted on recognition and she stretched her legs out and tumbled to his side. He heard the deep sigh come from her and saw her eyes searching his face with a hint of satisfied smugness in their depths. "A fine way to wake up, lass," Canyon murmured. She offered him a smile of undisguised satisfaction.

He sat up, leaned back against the warm wall of the cave, the fire still giving off smoldering heat, and

Blueberry curled against him once more. The first light of dawn showed itself at the mouth of the cave and Canyon smiled down at her as he stroked the peach-blond hair. He put his head back, her softness against him. All the pain and peril had been put aside in the sweet magic of her wanting. In the quiet moment he knew memories that reached out from another time, another place, an ocean away, and he realized that the beautiful moments are beyond place or time.

His voice lifted, soft sounds of a song rising in a firm, clear tenor.

Blueberry pushed up to gaze at him, full cupped breasts hanging beautifully, her nakedness somehow pure as driven snow. "Go on," she said.

"Never heard of a song for a girl named Blueberry." Canyon smiled. "But it's not the name, it's the song that counts, and I remember a ballad that'll do well for now and for you."

"Sing for me," she murmured, and looked magnificently lovely.

He lifted his voice again, the clear, firm tenor circling through the quietness of the cave.

I know a valley fair,
    Eileen Aroon,
I know a cottage there,
    Eileen Aroon,
Far in that valley's shade,
  I know a tender maid,
    Flower of the hazel glade,
    Eileen Aroon.

Who in the song so sweet,
    Eileen Aroon,
Who in the dance so fleet,
    Eileen Aroon,

Dear are her charms to me,
Dear are her laughter free,
Dear as her constancy . . .
Eileen Aroon . . .

He let the song trail off and held Blueberry to him
as the sun touched the mouth of the cave with a long,
probing yellow finger. "Time to put on clothes and
have a look outside," he said as he pulled the slender
figure to her feet.

"Let's look outside first," Blueberry said, and he
shrugged as he walked toward the cave entrance. She
followed on his heels to stand beside him as he halted
and surveyed the outside. The morning sun flooded the
hills, which were strangely peaceful and still. A few
new mounds of earth stretched across the bottom of
the nearest hill and a dip in the land below was now
flatter and higher. But to someone just arriving on the
scene, it would seem that nothing much had happened,
the contours of the hills different yet not discernibly
so. Except for the softness of the earth, Canyon noted.
"How long before it'll be hard enough to ride on?"
Blueberry asked.

Canyon squinted at the sun and drank in the heat of
it against his body. "I'd guess about noon," he said,
and felt Blueberry's hand come up to press against his
buttocks.

"I told you it wasn't time to put on clothes," she
murmured, and began to walk him backward into the
cave.

"The thin woman of Inis Magrath was right." Canyon smiled and Blueberry's frown was a question.
"She was a woman of the greatest wisdom, according
to Irish legend, a keeper of truths far beyond the wisdom of mere mortals. She said Man is God's secret,
Power is Man's secret, and Sex is woman's secret."

Blueberry drew him down to the bedroll. "I don't know anything about the thin woman of Inis Magrath, but I do know about Blueberry Hill," she said, a wise little smile toying with her lips.

"That'll do just fine," Canyon murmured as his mouth found hers and the cave became their own world again.

6

The sun hung directly overhead in the noon sky when Canyon dressed and waited for Blueberry to finish. She followed as he led the palomino from the cave, stepped carefully on the hillside, and then let the horse move forward. The earth was still soft but no longer clinging and clutching. He climbed onto the horse and rode a dozen yards back and forth on the hillside before he nodded in satisfaction. He was about to turn to Blueberry when he heard her excited cry. She pointed down to the bottom of the hill and he saw the brown form standing between two new mounds of earth.

"It's all right," she said. "At least it seems all right."

"Go down and have a closer look. I'll wait here," Canyon said. He swung from the palomino as Blueberry scurried downhill. She halted beside the horse, pausing to examine the animal's legs and lead it in a small circle before climbing onto the saddle. She rode up the hill to Canyon and he watched the horse's legs and feet as it climbed the still-soft earth. There was no limp, no sign of a pulled muscle, though the hoofprints left were deeper than they'd be by the day's end. "I'd say you were both lucky," Canyon remarked when she reached him.

"It was lucky. You're the reason I'm here," Blueberry said.

"One good turn deserves another," Canyon answered as he pulled himself onto the palomino. "Let's do some riding, lass."

She stared out at the hills as she fell in beside him. "We'll never pick up wagon tracks now," she murmured.

"Don't expect to, not around here. But we know which way the tracks were headed before the rains came. We'll keep on that way," Canyon said.

"But they could've turned off anywhere."

"They could have, but maybe we'll get lucky. Sanderson will have to wait till the day's end before the ground's hard enough to support heavy wagons. Night'll be on him then, so the chances are he'll stay wherever he is till morning. I expect we'll pick up almost a day on him."

Canyon spurred the palomino up the hillside. He had almost reached the top when he saw the long, trenchlike hole to the right, and he swerved the horse toward it only to rein up short as he reached it. The frown dug deep into his brow as he peered into the hole. It was filled with bodies in the stiffened positions of death.

Blueberry gasped as she came up to him. "My God, it's a mass grave."

"It's open only because the rain and mud slide washed away the covering soil," Canyon said. "Twenty-four bodies, I count."

"Who'd bury all these people way up here?" Blueberry wondered aloud.

"I don't know," Canyon said. "They're all white men."

"The Indians did this?"

"No, they don't do this kind of burying," Canyon

said. "Something damn funny about it, though. It's no proper grave. It looks as though they were just dumped in and covered up." He stared at the grisly scene for a moment longer as a strange grimness curled inside him, unformed and undefined yet very much there. "We won't learn anything more standing here and we've our own fish to fry," he said.

At the top of the hill he saw a steep passage that led into the high hills. At the end of the passage he turned up another one and kept climbing into high hill land until he finally pulled to a halt on a stone ledge that afforded an almost unbroken view of the hills below.

"You can't be looking for wagon tracks from here," Blueberry said.

"No, I'm letting the land speak to me."

"Is it going to tell you where they are?"

"Not exactly, but it'll pretty much tell me where they aren't." Canyon pointed to where the hills led north. "Too steep," he grunted. "Not a passage a wagon could negotiate for long. Now look south. Every passage is narrow, much too narrow for a heavy wagon. They'd not be turning east, we know that, so we're left with west. Let's ride."

He sent the palomino downhill and west and toward a wide, thick stand of hackberry, red maple, and box elder. It was a wide, long forest, perfect for taking refuge from a storm, and when he reached the lower hills, he rode due west as the day slid to an end. He rode another hour through the darkness and finally halted for the night. Blueberry folded herself tight against him and the night passed quickly.

When morning came, he found a stream to wash and a clump of wintergreen berries on which to breakfast. He set a fast pace until the sun grew too hot. Then they slowed and rode along the edge of the treeline, where he could have shade and yet keep his eyes on the terrain. He'd gone perhaps another five miles when he spotted the wheel tracks that emerged from the trees ahead. He heard Blueberry's little excited gasp.

"Only a few hours old," Canyon said. Now they followed the tracks at a fast trot. The trail moved crossways along the hills and then turned down into a valleylike strip of land with high, tree-thick ground on both sides. The tracks were very new now, little drops of moisture still glistening in the ruts made by the wheels. The valleylike strip of land rose, the wagon wheel tracks climbing up with it.

Canyon had just started to follow when the fusillade of shots rang out. He cast a glance at Blueberry and saw the fright leap into her face. He motioned for her to follow him as he raced the palomino up the side of the depression and into heavy tree cover.

He held the pace as he raced upward inside the trees and finally swerved to move to his left, where the sounds of gunfire had grown more furious. Blueberry was still close behind him. He dodged his way through the thick tree cover until he reined to a skidding halt to peer down at the scene just below. The wagons were stopped and he saw some ten attackers pouring bullets down on them from two sides. Four of the men with the wagons were already lying dead—some on the wagons, others crumpled at the base of the wheels. Two more went down as the attackers circled.

"Can't we do something?" Blueberry whispered.

"We're too late. We'd only wind up getting ourselves killed, too," Canyon said. He swung to the ground.

Blueberry was beside him instantly as he dropped to one knee. "This must be a much worse attack than any of the others. They're killing everyone," Blueberry said.

"Not Sanderson," Canyon said, and drew a sharp glance.

"What's that mean?" she asked.

"I don't know, but he's big enough for a blind man to hit." Canyon watched the man where he crouched behind the rear wheel of the last wagon as bullets flew all around him. A frown dug into Canyon's brow as the last two of the men with the wagons fell dead and Sanderson pushed himself to his feet and stepped forward. But no hail of bullets smashed into his huge shape. Instead, the shooting came to an end and Sanderson waved one tree-trunk arm into the air. The attackers came forward to form a semicircle around the wagons.

"Start digging," Sanderson called out. "Hurry it up. I'm running late now."

The frown on Canyon's brow dug still deeper as the attackers pulled shovels from their saddle gear and began to dig a long trench. Two of them dismounted and began to drag the slain men forward.

"That mass grave we found," Blueberry breathed.

"The crews of the other shipments." Canyon nodded. "There were seven shipments so far so there's got to be other trenches."

"Good God," Blueberry breathed, her eyes riveted on the scene before her as, the trench completed, the eight men of the wagon crew were unceremoniously dumped in.

"That's why he changed to a new crew each shipment," Canyon said. "It wasn't just to make himself look conscientious. He had to because he kills off the crew of each shipment so there'll be nobody around to talk."

"Billy," Blueberry bit the name out with a harsh gasp of breath. "That's why he never came back. He was killed with the others on the last shipment." Canyon glanced at her as he heard her rise, spin, and yank the rifle from her horse. "That bastard," she hissed. She started to raise the gun when he leapt, yanked her hand away from the trigger, and pulled the rifle from her grasp. He clapped one hand over her mouth.

"Stop it," he hissed, and pushed her to the ground. "That won't help Billy and it sure as hell won't help us." He held her still as she glared back, but she finally blinked and he saw the moment of rage drop away from her. He took his hand from her mouth and helped her back to one knee beside him. "Things still don't fit. I want to see the rest of it," he said.

They turned back to peering through the trees. The shallow trench had been covered with the soil dug from it and patted down so it would be unnoticable to anyone casually riding by.

"There's got to be more," Canyon murmured, and the words had just fallen from his lips when the wagons appeared, moving down from the trees on the hillside. Four seed-bed wagons, he counted, with extra heavy sides, drawn by two-mule teams and each loaded with tarpaulin-covered boxes. They lined up alongside Sanderson's wagons as Canyon watched, his curiosity spiraling.

Sanderson moved quickly, barking orders as he paced back and forth directing operations as the covers were taken from the chests of silver and the silver dumped in neat piles on the ground. The mule-drawn wagons were uncovered next, the long boxes filled with flat stones, Canyon saw, and the men began transferring the stones into the emptied silver chests.

They filled each chest three-quarters full with the stones, then poured enough silver back to take up the top quarter of the chest. "They've been making off with three-quarters of every shipment," Canyon said, grudging admiration in his voice. "Clever, very clever.

It's all coming together now. When the wagons get to the storage area, they're checked, of course. The opened chests look right, and even if they dig some, the top quarter of each chest is silver so they pass inspection easily.''

"But the government is really storing away chests that are three-quarters filled with stones,'' Blueberry finished.

"Which they'll find out when they start to use the silver, only it'll be too late then. Sanderson will be long gone with enough silver to buy himself a new country.'' Canyon paused to watch the slow and careful process of exchanging the silver for the stones and then adding back enough silver for each chest.

"He's been real smart,'' Canyon said, his eyes narrowed on the huge figure of Jake Sanderson. "If he'd let his raiders make off with entire shipments, it would've triggered an instant response. Maybe Washington would've ordered the army to ride herd on each shipment. That would've put an end to his whole scheme. So to avoid that, he faked small raids while he's really been siphoning off three-quarters of every shipment.''

"But Washington sent you. They must've suspected something,'' Blueberry said.

"They didn't suspect anything. They sent me to put a stop to the raids before they grew more serious,'' Canyon told her. "That's why Sanderson tried to have me ambushed and then sent me chasing after you. If I were riding the shipment, it'd wreck everything for him.'' He fell silent as the attackers climbed into the silver wagons to take the place of the assassinated crew while the rest of the men began to wheel the second four wagons away, now loaded with most of the silver. Canyon watched as the two-mule teams began to pull the wagons up the steep side of the hill and into the tree cover.

"They'll be taking it to wherever they're keeping it," he muttered, "while Sanderson and the others take the silver shipment to the storage depot."

"What do we do now?" Blueberry asked.

"We sure as hell can't attack either of them," Canyon said. "And we don't know where either place is."

"We can only follow one. But which one?" Blueberry said.

Canyon's jaw set in a grim line. "We're dammed either way, but it seems we have no choice. It has to be Sanderson. We have to nail him down first, when he reaches the storage place," he said, and pulled himself into the saddle. Blueberry rode beside him as he started through the trees. "We stay as far back as we can, just enough to keep them in sight," he said as he slowed, held back until the four wagons had almost disappeared into the distance.

He rode forward then, following, staying in the trees as much as possible. He saw the riders beside the last wagon peering in all directions as they rode. When they rolled into clear land and down a narrow passage, Canyon took the palomino higher into the hills to stay in the tree cover and saw the outriders were still nervously glancing behind and to each side.

"Let's ride apart," Canyon said to Blueberry. "Somebody looking back at the right moment could spot two horses together a lot easier than one. I'll move over to keep us about ten yards apart."

She nodded and he swerved to the left, counted off the distance, and then began to move forward again. He glanced across through the trees, glimpsed Blueberry, then saw her disappear in heavy foliage and appear again. But she was paralleling him, keeping back, he noted in satisfaction, and he returned his eyes to the wagons.

Sanderson moved them through paths that wandered across the hills, and the four wagons dropped completely from sight when they took a passage that led downhill behind a low ridge. But Canyon made no effort to hurry forward. They'd move into sight soon enough, he was confident, and he stayed back inside the tree cover.

When they reappeared, they were rolling down a trough between two hills. Canyon, staying on the high ground, followed. The trough stayed a straight pathway for over half a mile, and O'Grady kept his eyes on the wagons with but an occassional glimpse across to catch fleeting sight of Blueberry.

But the trees began to thin, he noted, and he knew they'd be losing the thick cover soon. They'd have to come into open land. He slowed the palomino to fall back farther. He'd gone perhaps another hundred yards when he heard the short, sharp cry, Blueberry's voice, surprise and fright in it. He spun the palomino to the right and raced the short distance, the Colt in his hand as he reached her and reined to a sharp halt. Two almost naked figures, on foot, their bows drawn and arrows pointed directly at Blueberry didn't move as he drew up. Blueberry sat frozen in place, her eyes wide with fear, and Canyon leveled the Colt at the nearest Indian, who wore a Pawneee wrist gauntlet. The Indian's black eyes flicked to him, but the drawn arrow stayed pointed at Blueberry.

Canyon's finger touched the trigger of the Colt, reluctant to shoot unless he'd no choice. A shot would still be heard by Sanderson. He shot a glance at the second Pawnee and saw the Indian hadn't moved either. Canyon kept the Colt leveled at the nearest Pawnee, ready to fire in a split second if he saw the man's fingers release the bow. A voice sounded directly behind him and Canyon's lips drew back in disgust as he swore under his breath. He half-turned in the saddle to see three more Pawnee, arrows pointed at him on drawn bows, while still another one came from the trees on his pony, his hand outstretched in an unmistakable gesture for the Colt.

Canyon measured the three arrows pointed at him. They'd not miss at that distance, he realized. He let the Colt fall from his fingers. One of the Indians instantly leapt forward and scooped it up.

Canyon swore at himself. His complete concentration had been on the wagons. A mistake, a very definite mistake. He wondered how long the Pawnee had been watching him and Blueberry. Not that it mattered much now, he snorted as three more Pawneee appeared on horseback. One took hold of the palomino's bridle, another pulled the reins from Blueberry's hands and brought her alongside the palomino. Wordlessly, they began to lead their captives away as Canyon dammed the devil's luck and his own carelessness.

7

"Where are they taking us?" Blueberry half-whispered as they were led back through the trees.

"I hope not all the way back to the main camp," Canyon answered.

"I guess we'll lose track of the wagons altogether now," she murmured.

"We could lose track of our heads, lass," he told her, and saw the panic leap into her eyes. He'd no desire to frighten her more, but it was time for facing the truth. His glance went to the Pawnee, sought to find a weak place, a brave riding casually, a gap in between riders. But he found nothing: the Pawnee were watching their captives with unflagging attention. The brave in the lead suddenly swerved to the right and the others followed, pushed Canyon along with them as Blueberry followed, and Canyon rode onto a square, flat section of land where another half-dozen Pawnee waited. He saw the heavy, hook-nosed face and the necklace of polished stones at once. "Thunderstone, Chief of the Flint Hills Pawnee," he muttered to Blueberry.

"Is he a friend of yours?" she asked with instant hope in her voice.

"I wouldn't say that exactly." Canyon smiled grimly. "But we've met."

The Pawnee chief moved his pony forward and his

coal-black eyes surveyed the big man on the palomino, went to the young woman and back to the palomino again. "The man with the fire in his hair," Thunderstone said. "Why do you still ride the Pawnee hills?"

"Not to harm the Pawnee," Canyon offered.

"All white man say the same when they are captured," Thunderstone said, and used sign language to emphasize his words. "You were given a chance to leave. You did not. Now you will pay." He flicked a finger and Canyon felt hands yanking him from the saddle. He was pushed against a sapling and rawhide thongs tied his arms and chest to the tree. He saw Blueberry's arms strapped behind her to another sapling. Then as the chief looked on, her shirt was pulled off, her skirt next, and finally she was naked against the tree.

One by one, the Pawnee passed in front of her, each going over her with his hands, each roughly fondling her body, and Canyon watched the fear build in Blueberry's eyes until suddenly she screamed and began to kick out. The screams only brought on raucous laughter and even rougher fondling as the Indians ran their hands up her inner thighs and grabbed at her legs as she tried to kick out. Blueberry was sobbing as much as screaming now and Canyon's glance went to Thunderstone to see the chief watching with the hint of a smile on his face.

Canyon lifted his voice in a shout. "Shut up," he screamed at Blueberry. "Shut up." He saw her look at him, incomprehension in her face. "You're making it worse for yourself," he said, and saw her swallow hard, pull strength from inside herself, and fight back the sobs. After a few moments more, the Pawnee left her alone and one fetched a small hide sack while others began to put pieces of twigs in it.

"What are they doing now?" he heard Blueberry ask.

"I don't know," Canyon said, counting the lie as a good deed. He knew full well what the Pawnee were doing. They were preparing to decide which of them would enjoy her first. He knew he had only one chance left to help Blueberry. And himself, he grunted, for he'd be next as soon as they'd had their way with her. One chance, if it were a chance at all, he grimaced. But the Pawnee chief had shown he'd bargain. Greed was more important than pleasure to him. And he was also not to be trusted, Canyon knew. But there was no other choice. He turned his eyes to Thunderstone while the braves began to kneel down around the sack, which was now filled with twigs.

"Is Thunderstone a chief without memory?" Canyon called out in Siouan, and he saw the Pawnee turn to him with a frown. Canyon repeated the question and added sign language to make it clear.

"A Pawnee chief has many memories," the Indian answered.

"Then Thunderstone will remember how I traded a fine horse and rifle for a worthless prisoner," Canyon said, and the Pawnee nodded slowly. "I can do more now, much more."

Thunderstone's face remained expressionless as he turned to stare at Canyon, but his coal-black eyes flickered. "Talk," he murmured.

"Many horses, many rifles, pistols, shells," Canyon said. "For the woman and myself." He repeated the offer again with sign language.

"How many?"

"Ten, more maybe," Canyon answered. "Clothes, blankets, many things to use at camp."

The Pawnee chief stayed silent while thoughts turned

in his mind, Canyon knew, the man's eyes flickering. "Where?" Thunderstone questioned.

"I will lead you," Canyon said. "Many horses you can trade." Canyon chose words carefully. "You will have to kill for them," he added, and saw the nod the Pawnee was quick to give. Canyon smiled inwardly. The condition was an incentive, as he'd thought it would be.

Thunderstone barked orders at the braves and two of them came to cut the rawhide thongs from around Canyon's wrists and chest.

"You will lead us," Thunderstone said.

"She comes along," Canyon answered, pointing to Blueberry.

"She stays here until you have proved you word," Thunderstone said.

Canyon shook his head. "She comes along," he insisted with more adamancy than he had a right to feel. But he knew the Pawnee well enough: the chief's appetite had been whetted. It was a time to stand firm.

"If I say no?" Thunderstone growled.

"I stay here with her. No horses, no guns, no blankets."

The Indian seemed to ponder. But Canyon was certain the chief's decision had already been made. Thunderstone finally gestured to one of the braves and Blueberry was cut loose. She immediately scooped up her clothes and put them on while flinging contempt at the watching Indians. Another brave brought Cormac and Blueberry's horse.

"You go. We ride behind," Thunderstone ordered.

Canyon swung into the saddle and waited for Blueberry to come alongside him. "My gun," he said to the Pawnee chief.

"When you take us to the guns and horses," Thunderstone said.

"I'm not coming all the way back here for it," Canyon pressed, and Thunderstone spoke to one of the braves in Caddoan. The Indian came up with the Colt and pushed it into the rawhide thong that circled his waist and held up his loincloth.

"He will give you your gun when the time comes," the Pawnee chief said, and turned away. Canyon moved the palomino off at a slow canter and Blueberry stayed beside him.

"Who are you taking them after?" she asked.

"The ones who attacked Sanderson," Canyon said. "I want Sanderson alive so he can tell where he has hidden the other shipments. Besides, the attackers will be moving slower with mule teams."

"But you'll lose all the silver, then," she said.

"No, the Pawnee won't care about the silver. They'll want guns, ammunition, clothes, blankets, anything they can use, and the pleasure of killing," Canyon told her.

"You expect they'll wipe out the men," Blueberry said. "And then they'll let us go."

"That was the bargain," Canyon said, and something in his voice drew a quick, sharp glance from Blueberry.

"You don't think they will," she commented.

"Let's just say I don't trust a Pawnee's word on anything," Canyon said. "I was buying time for us. This was the only way I could think of to do it. From here on we wait, watch, and hope we get a chance to make a break for it."

O'Grady broke off further talk as he saw the area where the attackers had first hit the shipment. He rode onto the flat space and picked up the tracks of the mule-drawn wagons they had led up the steep hillsides. The tracks were still fresh and clear; he followed and looked back, to see the Pawnee close at his

125

heels. The wagon tracks continued uphill until, at a ridge, they turned left and continued along high ground for another mile. They turned unexpectedly, down into a wide flat passage at the bottom of three hills, and suddenly the tracks became the wagons, four of them moving with heavy slowness, a driver on each and an outrider alongside. They were moving along with unconcern.

Canyon halted and gestured to Thunderstone.

The chief rode up, looked below, and nodded, a faint smile of anticipation playing around his lips. Thunderstone grunted orders at four of his braves, and the Indians moved up to flank Blueberry and Canyon on both sides while the others followed their chief forward. Thunderstone halted at the edge of the slope, lifted one arm, and screamed a wild, whooping cry that was instantly echoed by the others.

As Canyon watched, the redmen swooped down on the wagons, breaking up into three small groups. One of the drivers never had time to recover as two arrows pierced him at once and he toppled from the seat of the wagon. Others tried to take cover, but the Pawnee were firing arrows in clusters from three directions. One of the Indians went down and three more of Sanderson's men. Another rider took down one Pawnee before he was pierced by three arrows.

Blueberry watched the unequal battle below with horror, but Canyon's eyes went to the four Pawnees who flanked them.

All were intent on the attack, half-smiles on their faces as they took part from a distance, and Canyon leaned over to Blueberry. "It's now or never," he said. "The flies are concentrating on the honey. When I go, you come after me and stay flat in the saddle." She nodded and he flashed another glance at the braves. They were all still intent on the battle below.

Canyon saw his Colt still in the leather waistband of the nearest Pawnee. He moved the palomino sideways a few steps, came closer to the Indian, whose eyes were still following the end of the battle below. Canyon measured distances again, and then, his arm lashing out with the speed of a cougar's strike, he yanked the gun from the Indian's waist, brought it up, and fired, all in one unbroken motion.

The Indian's rib cage exploded in a show of red, but Canyon was already swinging the gun around, firing again, and one of the Pawnee on the other side flew from his saddle. "Ride," Canyon yelled at Blueberry as he flattened himself over the palomino's neck and sent the horse into a full gallop. It had all taken perhaps two seconds and the other two Pawnee were still recovering as Canyon streaked along the ridge with Blueberry chasing after him.

He glanced back past Blueberry to see the two Pawnee now giving chase. He stayed low as an arrow whistled past his head. He swerved the palomino sharply to the right and Blueberry followed, but her horse turned more slowly and Canyon saw the nearest Pawnee almost atop her. He reined up, lifted the Colt, and fired. The Indian toppled facedown from his horse just as he reached for Blueberry. Fargo fired again and the fourth Pawnee took the bullet full in the chest, seemed to leap from his pony, and shuddered in midair before he dropped to the ground.

Canyon set off again with Blueberry on his heels. He realized the sounds of the battle below had ended. He headed away, took a steep hill upward almost without slowing, and glanced back to Blueberry. She nodded to him to show she was all right, and he continued to send the palomino uphill when a horseman flashed through the trees to his right. He glimpsed the Pawnee almost opposite him. Thunderstone had heard the shots from below and, his attack a success, had sent a rider up to help the others, instantly aware of what had happened.

Canyon leveled the Colt at the attacking horseman, started to pull the trigger when his ears caught the soft, swooshing sound of an arrow at his back. He ducked down but not before the arrow put a large crease across the back of his head. Dimly, he felt the Colt drop from his fingers. The world swam away and he felt himself go down, clutching the horses's blond mane to slow his fall. He felt his shoulder slam into the ground. The shock snapped away the grayness that had started to engulf him. Thunderstone had sent two of his braves from below, not one, Canyon realized with a kind of abstract bitterness as he saw the red-skinned figure hurtling at him from the pony.

He managed to get one knee up and the Pawnee landed with all his weight on it. Canyon saw the Indian's face twist in pain as his knee smashed deep into the man's solar plexus. The Pawnee fell away, gasping for breath as he rolled on his side. Canyon whirled, leapt forward, and drove his forearm into the Indian's throat with all his strength. He heard the man's gargled gasp as his larynx collapsed, but Canyon had only time to fling himself from his foe when the second Pawnee came at him. This time the Indian's leap caught him across the back of his shoulders and he felt himself driven flat, facedown into the ground. An arm came around his neck, clamped against his throat; Canyon tried to whirl and claw the arm away, but the Indian was strong and dug his feet into the ground.

O'Grady felt his breath fast become a gasped trickle when suddenly his body shuddered with the force of another blow. The Indian's arm pulled away from his throat. He whirled, drew in a deep breath, and saw the Pawnee fighting off a clawing, biting figure with peach-blond hair. Canyon pushed to his feet just as the Indian flung Blueberry aside, whirled, and O'Grady's pile-driver right smashed flush into the man's jaw. The Pawnee went down and lay still. Canyon turned to see Blueberry picking herself up, her cheek smudged with dirt. "An avenging angel." He grinned. "Take to the saddle, lass." '

"Will the rest come after us?" Blueberry asked as she raced beside him through the trees.

"Probably not. They'll be busy collecting all the things they want. But we'll take no chances." Canyon kept the palomino at a gallop until he was deep into a forest of red ash. He slowed and finally drew to a halt at the edge of a small stream. He dismounted and lay down on the ground, his face into the stream; he drew back with the cool water coating his skin. Blueberry used the stream to clean the dirt from her face and she finally turned on her back, her breasts lifting with each deep breath.

"How long can we keep cheating death, Canyon?" Blueberry asked.

"As long as we have to," he answered. "We're not finished yet. We have to go back to trailing Sanderson and the other wagons until we reach the storage place."

"Then we can blow apart his whole scheme once and for all," Blueberry said.

"But it won't be a cakewalk, lass. We can't let him see either of us. We can't go in and start to convince people. If we do, he'll see us for sure and take off before we have a chance to nail him down. We have to take him by surprise so he can't run." Canyon rose to his feet and pulled Blueberry up with him. "The first thing is to pick up his trail. We'll be taking the long way back."

Blueberry riding beside him, O'Grady moved

through the hills in a wide circle, his eyes ceaselessly scanning the forest land and the hills. When he finally circled back downhill to the trough of land where the wagons had gone, twilight began to drift across the hills. This was the place where the Pawnee had taken them by surprise, and he moved down into the trough to see the wagon-wheel tracks were clear. He followed them along the trough until darkness descended.

They bedded down in a spot at the edge of the treeline alongside the trough. Canyon slept quickly, exhaustion on him, and Blueberry stayed hard against him until morning came, when they breakfasted on wild strawberries before picking up the trail again.

The wagon tracks crossed the hills straight west and once again dusk was descending when he reached a line of tall rocks and a wide passage between them. He slowed, edged forward through the passage, and halted when he saw a wide, flat area with a collection of buildings. He saw barracks buildings, a stable, and four heavy-sided structures that were plainly warehouses. He also saw barbed wire strung around the entire perimeter of the area and at least six sentries posted. What appeared to be a full platoon of troopers were drilling at one side of the space, and a wooden, slatted gate formed the only entrance.

"This is it, lass," Canyon murmured as he scanned the base again, his glance pausing at a small, neat building where the company flag flew overhead. "That'll be the commander's quarters," he said. "But there'll be no walking in to see him."

"Why not?" Blueberry frowned.

"This is a secret base. They didn't even tell me where it was in Washington. We walk in and we'll be held for questioning first, and Sanderson would learn about us being there damn fast. I'd guess he didn't arrive till late last night or this morning."

"So what do we do?" Blueberry asked.

"We have to be bold, even rough, cut corners and let the facts speak for themselves. This'll be a time when stones will talk." Canyon's eyes swept the barbed wire surrounding the base. "We wait till the place is asleep and then we sneak in."

"How do we do that?"

"To the right there's a spot. The bottom strand of the wire is strung high to go over some rocks. We can sneak under it there," he said.

He backed the palomino from the passage and turned up to a clump of black walnut on the top of a rise. He dismounted and sat down against one of the tree trunks as the dusk turned into night.

Blueberry came alongside him. He dozed and let the night grow long and in between he allowed himself the luxury of feeling satisfied. It had been a chase full of the unexpected, most of it unpleasant except for the peach-blond head that rested against his shoulder. Jake Sanderson had been a more devious and clever swindler than most, his scheme well-planned, elaborate, and ruthless. But it would soon be over, Canyon smiled. All he had to do now was to tear open the heart of it, a heart of stones . . . He almost laughed and let himself doze off again.

When he woke next, the night moon was high in the sky. "Time to finish things," he murmured to Blueberry. "We'll leave the horses here." She stayed beside him as Canyon began to move down through the passage. He dropped into a crouch at the other end when he neared the dark camp. He moved sideways, staying low, to the spot where he'd seen the barbed wire climb over the rocks. He halted when he reached it and silently cursed. The gap was smaller than it had seemed from a distance. He paused to scan the base again. The gate was closed and four guards were on duty there; another four sentries patrolled the back pe-rimeter of the area, but the camp was mostly dark and silent.

Canyon lowered himself to the ground and began to crawl under the wire, the sharp, cutting knots but a fraction from his face. Inching forward, he slithered, keeping his body tight to the ground. One knot of wire tore at the back of his shirt. But he finally cleared the wire, drew his legs after him, and once inside the wire, turned and beckoned Blueberry. She followed, her smaller frame passing more easily under the wire, un-til she finally rolled to his side. He rose and pulled her with him.

"Walk as if we belonged here," Canyon said, and she nodded, nervousness in her face. She linked her arm in his as he began to cross the open space with the long barracks building to one side.

He strolled toward the neat frame structure where the company flag flew, and when he was within six feet of the door, a figure stepped from the darkness, blue-uniformed, with rifle raised.

"Halt. Who goes there?" the guard demanded.

"I have to see the commander," Canyon said. "Of-ficial business."

"Commander Fisher's asleep. It's past midnight," the soldier said.

"Wake him up," Canyon said.

"I can't do that," the trooper said, plainly aghast at the thought. "You'll have to wait till morning."

"If you say so." Canyon shrugged and started to turn away. The soldier lowered his rifle. When Canyon whirled back, the Colt was in his hand, and in one step he had the gun held against the trooper's temple. "Take the rifle, Blueberry," he said, and she pulled the gun from the soldier, whose eyes were now wide with uncertainty and fear. "Now let's wake up the commander," Canyon said. Canyon's gun at his temple, the solider turned to the door and knocked, then knocked again. "Harder," Canyon growled, and the soldier obeyed.

A voice finally answered, more irritation than sleep in it. "What in hell is it?" the voice said.

"Trooper Jones, sir. Somebody to see you," the soldier answered.

"At this hour?" the voice barked, stronger now.

The door was pulled open and a tall, trim man, still in uniform, Canyon saw in surprise, peered out.

Canyon pushed the trooper into the house before him and Blueberry followed and pulled the door closed.

"What is this?" The commander frowned, and Canyon took the Colt from the trooper's temple.

"Sorry to come in like this, but there was no time for delays or proprieties," Canyon said. "I'm glad to see you're still dressed, Commander."

"I was in the back writing my monthly reports," the officer said.

O'Grady noted the major's insignia on his shoulders. Canyon took the card from his pocket and handed it to the major and waited as the man read from it.

"Canyon O'Grady, United States Government Agent," the officer said.

"Himself," Canyon answered, and saw Major Fisher cast a quick glance at Blueberry.

"I didn't know government agents went about their work with traveling companions," he said stiffly.

"They do when those companions are a help in the case." Canyon decided it was time to hurry things along. Major Fisher was a man suspicious, irritated, and plainly not about to accept strange behavior.

"Maybe you'd best explain why you come barging into my quarters at this hour of night at gunpoint, Mr.

O'Grady. How did you find this place, anyway?'' the commander said.

"It's a long story, but for now I'll skip to the important part. Most of the silver you've been storing here is nothing but stones. Jake Sanderson's been swindling the government out of most of every shipment.''

"That's preposterous,'' Fisher boomed. "We check each shipment that arrives.''

"Including the one that arrived yesterday?'' Canyon asked.

"Of course. It was all in order,'' the major snapped.

"That's what you think,'' Canyon said. "Suppose we go and have another look at that shipment right now.''

Fisher's frown stayed. "All right, dammit, let's do that,'' he agreed after a moment. "But I want Jake Sanderson there. We've dealt with him for over a year now and he deserves to hear this astonishing accusation in person.''

"Fine with me,'' Canyon said.

Major Fisher turned to the soldier. "Trooper Jones, take four men and bring Road Agent Sanderson to Warehouse Three. He's asleep in the barracks. I'll meet you at the warehouse.''

"Yes, sir,'' the trooper said with a salute, and hurried away.

Fisher fastened a sharp stare on the big, flame-haired man in front of him. "This is the wildest thing I've ever heard, O'Grady. It seems to me that Jake Sanderson and his men have been doing a fine job of limiting these raiders to only a few small boxes of silver, and now you say he's been swindling the government of most of it. How?''

"The raids are fakes, planned for effect. The real raids wipe out the entire wagon crew. Then most of the silver is replaced by stones. He leaves just enough to pass when you check the shipments,'' Canyon answered. "This young lady will back my words. We watched it being done on the last shipment.''

Major Fisher shook his head in disbelief. "Frankly, I find this impossible to accept. This would require a careful and clever operation of major proportions.''

"That's what it is, and now you can arrest Sanderson and put an end to it." Canyon followed the major as the man strode from his quarters and crossed to one of the warehouses. Four troopers stood guard outside the door. Fisher had the door opened and the lamps lighted, then ordered the four troopers inside with him.

Canyon swept the warehouse with a quick glance: rows of long boxes were piled atop one another and those wagons unhitched but still not unloaded were lined up to one side. It was but a few moments later when the detail of troopers arrived with the huge bulk of Jake Sanderson.

Canyon watched Sanderson's mouth fall open as he stared at him, his small eyes flicking to Blueberry for an instant as shocked astonishment draped the thick-jowled face. "How'd they get here?" Sanderson asked of the major.

"We followed you," Canyon answered, and enjoyed the shock that stayed in Jake Sanderson's face.

"You know these two?" Major Fisher asked Sanderson.

"I sure do," Sanderson said, licking his thick lips. "They used to work for me till I fired them. They swore they'd ruin my business. They tried a couple of times and failed."

Canyon saw the major staring at him. "This man showed me credentials that say he's a government agent," Fisher said.

Sanderson allowed a harsh guffaw. "Hell, he stole that," the huge man said.

"Good try, you stinking tub of lard," Canyon cut in, unhappy with the uncertainty he saw in the major's face. "This is wasting time," he said to Fisher. "He's trying to fast-talk his way out of it. Check out the shipment. That'll put an end to talk."

"Troopers, empty those chests onto the floor," Fisher said.

The soldiers immediately lifted the chests from the two wagons in the forefront. Carefully, they began to spill the silver onto the floor. Canyon's eyes went to Sanderson. The man watched with a half-sneer on his face. It was a good front, probably a desperate one. He had nothing left but to try to brazen his way through. Canyon returned his gaze to the silver that spilled out of the chests onto the floor. The soldiers worked steadily and soon there were three piles of gleaming silver on the warehouse floor and the chests were empty.

Canyon stared and felt the sharp, stabbing pain in the pit of his stomach. There were no stones, not a pebble. The chests had been filled from top to bottom with nothing but silver.

8

Was he having a bad dream? Canyon found himself wondering. Blueberry's short gasp of breath shattered the thought. He saw her stare at the silver with the same uncomprehending disbelief that had been in his own eyes. Something had gone wrong, terribly wrong. But how? What had happened? None of this made any sense, except in Sanderson's eyes, and the man's voice cut into his tumbling thoughts.

"I don't see any stones, do you, Major?" Sanderson said, his voice thick with sarcasm.

Major Fisher's voice sounded next, sheathed in ice. "You have anything to say, Mr. O'Grady?"

"I saw it, the whole thing. We both did," Canyon said, nodding to Blueberry. He met the harsh skepticism in the major's eyes and all he could do was to offer a helpless shrug. "The other wagons," he said. "Where's the rest of the shipment?"

"There were only two wagons this trip. It was a small shipment, Jake explained," the major said.

"There were four wagons," Canyon almost shouted. "Four wagons. Where are the other two?"

Jake Sanderson's voice cut in. "How long are you going to listen to this, Major? They're liars, both of them. What more proof do you want?"

"Take this man's gun," Major Fisher ordered, and

one of the troopers pulled the Colt from Canyon's holster.

"Dammit, everything I've told you is true," Canyon said. He heard himself half-choke in frustration. "I don't know what he did or how he managed to pull it off or how he even knew to be ready, but he's swindling you."

Major Fisher's face was made of granite. "Take these two into the guardhouse, separate cells," he ordered his men, and Canyon felt the rifles prod him in the ribs. "Passing yourself off as a government agent could get you ten years at hard labor alone, mister," the major added.

"I am a government agent, dammit," Canyon shouted. "While you're wasting time finding that out, that man will be off with everything he's stolen this far, and that's plenty."

"Lock them up," Fisher said.

Canyon felt the rage inside him as he saw the silent triumph in Sanderson's fleshy face. O'Grady was led from the warehouse, Blueberry beside him with three more troopers.

The guardhouse was situated at the far end of the barracks, three small cells with a place for a trooper to stand duty. Canyon was pushed into one cell, Blueberry into the adjoining one. The doors were slammed shut and a young trooper took up a position just outside the guardhouse where he could see in through a small window in the door.

Canyon turned to meet Blueberry's shrug. "I'm still wondering if I'm dreaming," she said. "Everything's turned upside down. Sanderson's supposed to be in here, not us."

"He turned it all around on us," Canyon said. "But how did he know to do it? I can figure out the mechanics. He took the silver from the four wagons and loaded into two after dumping the stones out, then showed up with only two. But why? How'd he know to do it? Had he changed plans? Did he decide on some last-minute move and we fell into it?''

"Whatever it was, it got him off the hook and us in here," Blueberry said.

"It did more than that. Sanderson knows that sooner or later the major will find out I'm who I said I am. That means he knows his operation is over. He's going to take off with everything he has so far. That's what I have to stop."

Blueberry gazed around her. "I'd say you're ignoring facts."

"We have to get out of here before daybreak," Canyon said. "That's not more than a few hours away."

"You have a magic carpet somewhere?"

"No, but I've immense faith in the compassion of young army troopers," Canyon said, and he began to remove his belt. He motioned to Blueberry when he finished, and she came toward the bars between the cells. "You lay down there, right against this cell. Facedown, as if you've fainted."

Blueberry lay down on the floor, one leg hanging limply, her body in a half-curve. Canyon turned to the front of the cell and began to kick at the bars. He saw the trooper outside turn to peer in through the window, and he motioned frantically to the man. The soldier opened the door, the rifle in his hands.

"Get in here. Something's happened to her. She just collapsed," Canyon said.

The trooper rushed in, took a key from a wall peg, and opened the door of Blueberry's cell. He set his rifle down as he bent over, dropped to one knee to peer at the young woman's apparently inert form. Canyon reached both hands between the bars as the soldier still bent low over Blueberry.

"Can you hear me?" the trooper asked of her. He started to say something more when the belt looped around his neck and Canyon yanked hard. The soldier fell against the bars, the belt holding his neck in a looping vise as Blueberry jumped to her feet.

"Now, I don't want to hurt you, lad," Canyon said. "Don't do anything to make me." He looked up and saw Blueberry had already taken the key and hurried around to unlock the door of his cell. "Where's my gun, lad?" Canyon asked.

"Top drawer, desk by the door," the soldier said in a strained wheeze.

Canyon heard the cell door open, but he still kept the belt tight around the trooper's neck. "Take his rifle and close the door to the cell," he said to Blueberry. He waited until she ran back, scooped the gun up, and slammed the cell door shut before he pulled the belt loose. The soldier slid to the floor, one hand rubbing his throat. Canyon dashed from the cell and found his gun in the desk drawer, glanced back at the trooper, who was pulling himself to his feet. "Don't let this change your mind about chivalry, lad. Always go to the aid of a lady in distress." Canyon hurried from the guardhouse with Blueberry.

He halted outside, stayed pressed against the wall, and scanned the base. The sentries were patrolling the perimeters, their attention on the darkness beyond. "We'll leave the same way we came," Canyon said, and began to edge his way around the buildings until they reached the rocks and the barbed wire. He slid his way through again, with equal care, and waited while Blueberry slipped through. "They'll know we're gone within an hour, maybe sooner. That'll depend on how loud the trooper can yell. Meanwhile, we get the horses," he said.

"Then, what?" Blueberry asked as she hurried

along beside Canyon, taking two steps for every one of his long-legged strides.

"We wait and watch. It's my guess Sanderson will be leaving in the morning. When he does, we'll follow him," Canyon said.

"Won't the major have a squad out trying to hunt us down? I mean, waiting around might get us back in his guardhouse."

"I'm wagering he won't send a squad out after us. His job is to protect the silver in those warehouses, and that means keeping his troops there," Canyon said as they reached the horses. He swung onto the palomino and sent the horse into a steep climb at once. He turned and halted in the trees at the edge of a ledge that let him look down onto the base. He dismounted, sat down against a tree, and forced his body to relax as he waited for the new day to dawn.

His eyes narrowed in thought as he rested, and Blueberry searched his face as she sat beside him. "Still thinking about Sanderson and the silver, aren't you?" she asked.

"Yes, I want to know why he didn't take the wagons in as usual," Canyon said. "But I'm sure of one thing: he's going to head for wherever he has the stolen silver stored. He's sure I'm on my way to get word to Washington, and that'll mean the end of his operation."

"Maybe that's what you ought to do," Blueberry said.

"No, that'd take far too long. He'd be gone with everything by then. I'm going after him and he'll talk before I'm through with him," Canyon said.

They waited in silence until the sun began to come over the hilltops. The base below took on shape in the new day, tiny figures moving across the area, only their blue uniforms distinguishable. But as the sun rose full into the sky, Canyon saw the warehouse door open and the two wagons emerge. Five un-uniformed figures climbed into the wagons and he made out the oversize girth of one of them. "He's got his crew and the wagons," Canyon muttered grimly. "I'd forgotten about the crew going back with him. But he'd have to do that and take the wagons to keep things looking right."

Canyon watched as a uniformed figure crossed over the talk to Sanderson for a moment. That would be the major, Canyon realized. He watched the two wagons begin to roll through the gate and out of the base. He stayed on the ledge, glimpsed the wagons move along the road, lost sight of them for a few moments as they were blocked by the rocks, and then picked them up again as they turned into the hills.

"Let's ride," he said as he climbed onto the palomino and began to drift through the trees in the same direction Sanderson and the wagons were going. They crossed his path some half-mile on. He slowed, let them climb higher into the hills before he swung in behind them. Sanderson turned the wagons east when they were halfway up a long hill, and followed a trail that cut across two smaller hills.

Canyon's brow creased as the land suddenly began to look familiar. The wagons made another turn upward and Canyon spurred the palomino after them. "I'll be dammed," he muttered.

Blueberry began to ask him a question when she saw the answer appear before her eyes as Sanderson halted beside the four wagons and the stripped-naked bodies. "This is where the Pawnee attacked," she gasped.

"How'd he know?" Canyon hissed, the question an echo of the one he had asked inside the storage warehouse. "He was far away, on his way to the storage base. How'd he know, dammit?"

"He came to collect the silver in those wagons," Blueberry said as they watched the four men transfer to the loaded wagons and begin to prod the mule teams forward.

"Of course. He wouldn't leave it here to go to waste," Canyon said. "He was prepared to make a fool and liar out of me at the warehouse, and he knew to come here. There has to be a connection. I'm going to find out if it's the only thing I do."

Canyon, his lips a thin line, moved the palomino forward again as the wagons began to climb, the mules struggling against the steepness of the hill.

"He didn't do anything about his men who were killed." Blueberry frowned. "He didn't even look at them, much less bury them. Hasn't he any sense of decency?"

"He keeps it hidden," Canyon spit out.

They slowed as he saw the wagons reach a place where the hill leveled off. They turned to the right, traveled along a line of flat ground with only a few trees on it, and turned again to where a rock formation rose up. Canyon saw high, steep-sided rocks directly behind a series of smaller boulders where two caves came into view, both with tall entrances. A line of box elder ran along one side of the path to the rocks and Canyon brought the horses into the trees before following farther. He drew closer, almost opposite the last of the wagons when it reached the rocks and drew to a halt.

O'Grady saw four men, each carrying a rifle, emerge from one of the cave entrances. He halted to watch as the men put down their rifles and began to help the four wagonmen unload the boxes and carry the first one into the cave. "Nine, including Sanderson. We'll have to wait and pick our time," Canyon muttered.

"Ten," a voice said from behind him, and Canyon's lips pulled back in a grimace. He turned to see the man and the rifle aimed directly at his back. "Throw your gun down, real slow," the man said, and Canyon eyed the rifle again and decided to obey. Even a blind man couldn't miss at so close a range. "Now, you and the girlie move forward," the man said, and Canyon exchanged glances with Blueberry.

"So much for picking our time," she commented, not without a trace of accusation in her tone.

Canyon rode out of the trees, Blueberry a half-step behind, and saw Jake Sanderson turn, his eyes growing as wide as they could first, then his fleshy face folding itself into a grin.

"Look what I found," the man called from behind.

"I'll be dammed," Sanderson said as he moved forward. "Now, isn't this a nice surprise? Get off your horses."

Canyon swung to the ground along with Blueberry, who remained at his side as Sanderson stepped closer and the others began to gather around.

Jake reached out, seized Blueberry by the arm, and flung her to the side, a spinning motion with enough force to send her sprawling. "I'll get to you later, honey," he muttered, his eyes boring into Canyon. The triumphant smile slid across his fleshy face again. "You've just put me back in business, O'Grady. Here I was going to fold up and run for it, but there's no need for that yet. I can get me at least another six shipments."

"Greed is a sin, you know," Canyon said. "It's led to the downfall of many a good man, to say nothing of the likes of you."

"You've a big mouth for a man in your position, Agent O'Grady," Sanderson snarled.

"I know. I've never learned my manners. A failing," Canyon said. "But then, you've been riding on the thin edge of luck, such as back at the warehouse."

"Surprised the shit out of you, didn't it?" Jake Sanderson laughed.

"It did that," Canyon admitted. "It seemed as if you were expecting me, and I can't put that together."

"I was." Sanderson laughed. "That man behind you was riding point for my wagons when you brought the goddamn Pawnee down on them. He was higher up in the hills and he saw you with them. He knew he'd only get himself killed trying to help the others, so he ran after me. He caught up to me a few hours before I reached the storage base."

"And you guessed I'd be coming after you next, so you made a fast switch with the silver," Canyon said.

"It worked just the way I figured it would. I think I enjoyed the look on your face most of all." Jake Sanderson laughed triumphantly. "And now we have to finish our work and then we'll finish with you and the little lady." He turned to the man who'd come up behind them. "Watch them. If they move, kill them," he snapped, and turned away to supervise the unloading of the wagons.

His men worked quickly, carrying and pushing the long boxes into the cave, and they had just finished when Canyon heard the low, rumbling sound of horses at a full gallop.

Sanderson heard it a moment after and whirled, his fat face darkened with surprise. "Get up on a rock and see what's going on," he ordered, and two of the men quickly clambered up the boulders that lined the face of the caves.

Blueberry glanced at Canyon, her eyes echoing her lips. "Wild horses?" she murmured.

"No. Too heavy a sound. Horses wearing shoes," Canyon said.

The shout interrupted him. "Jesus, it's the damn

army," one of the men on the rocks called. "Must be half a platoon. They're comin' this way."

"Shit," Jake Sanderson barked as his men jumped down from the rocks. He whirled and came at the big red-haired man, a snarl contorting his fleshy face. "This more of your shit?" he spit out.

"Not guilty. I'm as surprised as you," Canyon said honestly. "But not nearly as unhappy."

"Into the cave. They go with us," Sanderson barked, and Canyon began to run with the others, Blueberry a few paces behind as two of the men prodded them with their rifles. In the cave, Sanderson whirled at him and gestured to one side of the cave. "Over there," he ordered. "Get down by the wall." He yanked Blueberry with him and flung her down against the opposite wall. "Watch them," he ordered one of the men. "The rest of you get boxes up front."

Jake helped as the men began to shove and lift the long boxes of silver and stack them across the mouth of the cave. They were no snug fit and there were plenty of gaps between the boxes, but they still made a formidable wall.

"Get ready," Sanderson ordered, and the others crouched down behind the boxes, rifles and six-guns ready to fire.

Canyon shifted under the eyes of the man guarding him, found a spot where he could see outside through a space between two of the boxes. Only another minute passed before he saw the troopers charge into sight from the road below, Major Fisher in the lead. Canyon saw the major skid to a halt, and leap from his mount as he barked orders at the troopers who followed. The squad dispersed instantly, the soldiers diving for cover on both sides, army carbines in hand. Canyon tossed a glance at Blueberry and saw she had edged closer to him.

"I never expected to see the cavalry, much less be saved by them," she said.

"Don't count your chickens," Canyon admonished.

"What brought them charging up here?" she asked.

"Dammed if I know," he said.

The major's voice broke off further conversation as he called from outside the cave and out of Canyon's sight. "Come out with your hands up," Fisher ordered.

His answer was a furious volley of gunfire from inside the cave, much of it slamming wildly into trees, Canyon saw. He half-rose to get a better view through the space between the boxes. The man guarding him paid more attention to the mouth of the cave.

"Hold up," Sanderson shouted, and his men stopped firing, the sudden silence almost loud.

"I'll give you one more chance," Major Fisher shouted. "Come out with your hands up."

"Fire," Sanderson snapped, and joined his men in another short but furious volley of gunfire. He ordered another halt from where he stood against the end of one of the boxes. "Come in and get us," he shouted.

There was no answer and Canyon dropped lower just as the troopers began to pour bullets through the mouth of the cave. It was a far heavier fusillade the army carbines laid down than anything Sanderson's men had fired, and Canyon saw the pieces of wood sent splintering from the boxes and the stone chips fly from the sizable number of bullets that reached into the cave.

"Fire back," Sanderson shouted, and his men obeyed, most rising to pour shots over the tops of the boxes or through the spaces between them.

But the major hadn't slowed his fusillade. Instead, he'd ordered a furious volley of overlapping fire, and Canyon looked up as two of Sanderson's men went down and another screamed in pain as he fell clutching his shoulder. Canyon saw Blueberry, lying flat against the wall, arms over her head, as bullets pinged into the rock sides of the cave above her.

"Keep firing, dammit," Sanderson yelled as he darted to the other side of the cave behind the boxes.

The man who had been guarding O'Grady rushed forward to join the others firing back. Sanderson's men paused to reload while the volleys from outside continued to pour in as the major had his men firing in rotation.

Unable to see his targets, Fisher was laying down a blanket of furious gunfire that had its own effectiveness. One of Sanderson's men rose to fire over one of the boxes and was cut down immediately as three bullets all but tore his head off.

"Fire, fire," Sanderson kept shouting, but Canyon saw the men exchange nervous glances when suddenly the trooper's gunfire shifted focus. Volley after volley of bullets was aimed upward and slammed into the stone ceiling just over the boxes. Stone chips began to rain down, but more damaging, a cloud of rock dust fell, thick, white, choking dust that descended in a small cloud. Even though he was back a half-dozen feet, Canyon felt the fine white rock dust seeping into his throat and he closed his mouth to breath through his nose.

"Fire," Sanderson still screamed through the dust that was quickly filling the front of the cave.

"Shit, I can't breathe," one of the men shouted back.

"Fire, damn you," Sanderson screamed as another fusillade slammed into the rock ceiling to dislodge more white dust.

Canyon almost smiled. He was quickly gaining new respect for Major Fisher. It took another leap as the major plainly ordered his troopers to redirect their fire again, and as Sanderson's men half-rose to fire, they ran into a hail of bullets no longer aimed at the ceiling. Two more went down through the mist of white dust.

"No more for me," he heard one of the men say through the dust.

"Me neither," another answered as he coughed.

"All right, all right," the first one shouted at the top of his lungs. "Hold your fire. We quit." He yelled the words again and they finally sounded outside over the continuing hail of bullets.

Canyon heard the trooper's volley of shots begin to dwindle away and he lifted his head even as he wondered what had made Sanderson fall silent. He looked across at Blueberry and saw only an empty space. Alarm and anger spiraling inside him, Canyon leapt to his feet and peered through the white dust cloud that was now settling. He saw what was left of Sanderson's men standing by the boxes, but the huge form of Jake Sanderson himself had vanished.

"Come out with your hands up," he heard the major call from outside, but Canyon was already racing for the back of the cave. His eyes scanned the uneven wall as he reached it, his lips forming the oaths that thundered inside him. He pressed his hands against the rock wall as he moved across its protrusions and clefts, and he was almost at the end when he spotted the narrow, tall passageway that appeared in the wall. It was barely large enough for Jake Sanderson to fit his bulk into it, Canyon saw as he squeezed himself in and began to rush down the darkness of it. It was plain that Sanderson had been the only one to know it was there.

Canyon felt his shoulders scraping the stone sides. The passage stayed narrow as it wound its way through the rock, a fissure from a million years ago when the rock formation was born. But suddenly he glimpsed a faint glow of light and he raced forward. Sanderson had taken Blueberry with him as insurance, of course. It was his way to always have a way out, to always have a last card in the hole, a part of his self-serving cleverness.

The glow of light grew stronger, became daylight, and Canyon saw the end of the passage ahead. He increased speed and emerged from the passage to see an uneven terrain well covered by brush and low trees, mostly cockspur hawthorn. It was easy to see where Sanderson had dragged Blueberry through the high brush, branch ends broken and bruised, leaves still bent backward. O'Grady followed and realized he had no gun, no knife, no weapon at all. But there was no time for turning back to get one. Sanderson probably had a hiding place somewhere, maybe even a horse stashed away. That'd be in character, too. Canyon hurried after the trail through the brush.

The man had climbed across one of the brush covered hillocks and down the other side. O'Grady moved forward with an easy, long-legged stride. Sanderson would be pretty near out of breath by now and he'd have to rest his overstuffed body. Canyon was inside a cluster of trees when he spied the small, open space and the huge bulk half-sitting on a rock, Blueberry on the ground in front of him. Sanderson held her left wrist with a short length of rawhide. Canyon moved closer and dropped to one knee. He also saw the gun in the man's right hand.

The first thing was to get Blueberry away from him, to end the chance of his keeping her as a hostage. Canyon scanned the ground as he crept closer on soft steps. A section of broken branch, perhaps four feet in length, caught his eye, and he scooped it up. Both ends were broken and it was too thick to use as a lance. But it would have to do. All he needed was a moment of surprise. Blueberry would seize it and run, he knew.

Canyon moved forward again, the piece of branch in his hand. He dropped to one knee again where the trees and high brush ended, and he was not more than ten feet from Sanderson. He saw the man draw in a deep breath and start to push to his feet.

"Let's go, bitch," Sanderson growled. He yanked the rawhide around Blueberry's wrist. She came to her feet and he started off, his back to where Canyon crouched.

"Now or never," Canyon whispered aloud, lifted the length of branch, and realized it would waver and probably go off course if he tried to throw it as a lance. He took it by one end, drew his arm back, and used all the strength of his powerful arm and shoulder muscles to send the piece of wood sailing end over end through the air.

Sanderson heard the sound of it at the last minute, turned, tried to duck away, but the piece of wood caught him alongside the back of the head. He fell forward, stumbling, and landed on his hands and knees.

Blueberry was already racing away as Canyon charged from the brush, and she threw herself prone on the ground as she saw him. He landed on Sanderson's wide back as the man started to get up, and drove him forward again. This time the gun fell from Sanderson's hand and skittered away through the grass. Too far away to reach, Canyon saw, and he wrapped his arm around the man's neck. But Sanderson's neck hardly existed, his head fitting square onto his shoulders. With a bull-like roar, the huge figure rolled, carrying the object on his back with it, and Canyon felt himself thrown a half-dozen feet away. He landed on his side, rolled, and came up on his feet to see Sanderson's huge bulk charging at him.

"Son of a bitch," Sanderson roared as he charged.

Canyon set himself, measured the distance, and unleashed a left hook that landed flush on the jaw of the charging figure. It would have stopped most men in their tracks, but Sanderson's bulk and momentum carried him forward as though he hadn't been touched. Canyon spun himself sideways, crouched, and felt the man's weight slam into him. He tried to stay on his feet but was sent flying and hit the ground on one knee. He looked up to see Sanderson charging again, and he dived sideways as the small mountain thundered by. He rolled and rose.

Sanderson was turning to come at him again. But the tremendous left hook had not been entirely ineffective, Canyon saw. The man's jaw hung down in broken slackness. Sanderson came at him, his face a mask of fleshy rage. Canyon feinted, stepped in, and sank a tremendous right into the man's abdomen. It was not unlike hitting a giant pillow. Sanderson didn't even grunt. Canyon easily ducked a heavy arm that came at him, then another that came closer. He couldn't afford to be caught by one of those pile-driver blows, he knew, but he needed to somehow wear Sanderson down for his own blows to affect the man's huge bulk.

Jake charged again, this time moving with surprising quickness. Canyon had to duck as the blow whistled over his head. But he saw Sanderson suck in wind after the quick move, and he smiled. Sanderson had shown his weakness. Canyon began to move forward, feinted, and shot out a light left. Sanderson brushed it away and came forward with another pile-driver right. Canyon ducked away, came in again with his hands low, and Sanderson charged, swinging with both hands. Once more Canyon ducked lightly away.

The huge figure came at him again as Canyon seemed to be hesitant, attempting only tentative blows. Sanderson unleashed a left, right, and another left. Canyon darted in, but Sanderson tried a tremendous uppercut that caught nothing more than air. He followed with another right and left, then another as Canyon offered a target and was content to twist away. Sanderson was lunging now, blows that were great sweeping arcs, and Canyon heard his breath rasping in deep heaves.

Suddenly the huge man halted, tried to gasp in breath, and Canyon moved with lightninglike speed. His left and right caught Sanderson's already broken jaw and the man staggered backward, pain flashing in the folds of his face. But it was his eyes that Canyon watched with a slow grin. Sanderson had just realized what he'd let happen to him. He backed, tried to gulp in deep breaths as Canyon came in with a right feint, crossed a whistling left that split the man's brow open, followed with a right that smashed his nose into a claret smear. Sanderson staggered and Canyon stepped in low, aimed, and smashed a tremendous left hook, all his strength behind the blow. It caught the man just under his heart, battering through the layers of flesh. Sanderson's face went chalk-white. A long, rasping sound came from his lips as he fell to one knee, still rasping, then slowly collapsed onto his back. He lay rasping, his huge bulk giving off tiny shudders.

Canyon turned to clasp Blueberry to him as she ran into his arms.

She clung to him for a long moment and finally stepped back. "You all right?" she asked.

"I've been better." He smiled. "My arms hurt."

"I yelled when he grabbed me in the cave, but there was so much shooting going on I knew you didn't hear me," Blueberry said, and looked across at Sanderson's huge bulk where it lay on the ground. "Is he dead?"

"I don't know. Let's take a look." Canyon pushed Blueberry back as he walked over to the man. Sanderson lay still, a small mountain, his eyes closed in the fleshy face that was now a smear of red. His heart could've given out, Canyon realized, the strain and the tremendous blow he'd sent in could well have done the job.

O'Grady bent his head down to the huge, fat-covered chest to see if he detected a heartbeat. He caught the faint movement, started to lift his head up when Jake's huge arm encircled his throat, pulled him down against the massive chest, and he felt the grip already shutting off his breath. Canyon tried to claw the arm away, but it was impossible. His breath was being shut off fast. Swinging his body around, he dug his heels into the ground, arched his back, and used all the leverage and strength he had. But it was like trying to dislodge a mountain and he could hear his own rasping sounds.

O'Grady tried again, dug his heel in once more, and twisted the lower part of his body. This time Sanderson's bulk moved, turned half on its side. But the vise-like arm stayed and Canyon realized it was a kind of death grip, muscles and tendons locked in place. The world was beginning to go gray as O'Grady felt the last of his breath trickle away, and then, with strange dimness, he heard the shot and the arm around his neck suddenly grew limp. He clawed at it again, tore it away, and rolled across the ground. He came up on one knee to see Blueberry standing over the mountainous shape, the gun in both hands.

"Bastard," she sobbed. "Rotten bastard. This one's for Billy."

She shot again and the rest of Sanderson's head tore away. She turned, dropped the gun, and put her face into her hands. Canyon rose, ran to her, and pulled her with him as she shuddered. He held her until she stopped and looked up at him. She blinked and was dry-eyed. "I was right the other day," he said, and she frowned back. "An avenging angel. And a beautiful one at that. Let's go back, lass."

Her hand closed inside his as he began to lead the way back through the passage, into the cave. He saw the troopers moving the boxes turn in surprise. They stared at him as he walked outside to where Major Fisher's face flooded in surprise.

"My God," the officer said. "I didn't know you were in there."

"Surprise, surprise," Canyon said. "Sanderson's dead. He tried to get away through a passage out the other end."

Fisher looked at Blueberry for a long moment. "You all right, miss?" he asked, and Blueberry nodded.

"You came up with a surprise yourself, Major," Canyon said. "I sure as hell never expected to see you come charging up here."

"Wondering about that, are you?" Fisher smiled.

"That's putting it mildly," Canyon said.

"When they told me you'd gotten out of the guardhouse, I couldn't go back to sleep again. I tossed and turned and sat up finally, and suddenly I realized that the escape wasn't what kept me from going back to sleep," the major said. "I kept seeing the complete shock on your face, and on the young lady's, when those boxes were full of nothing but silver."

"That's putting it mildly again," Canyon said.

"I began to realize that you had honestly expected them to be three-quarters full of stones," Major Fisher said. "And then I realized that you'd never have suggested emptying the boxes in front of everyone if you'd been trying to get back at Sanderson as he suggested.

155

You'd have known better if you knew your story was hollow. Of course, at the time I thought you were just a brazen fool who'd gotten yourself trapped into more than you'd bargained for.'' Canyon allowed a half-smile and Fisher went on. ''When I began to have second thoughts, I decided to let Sanderson go on his way as he usually did. But this time, when I allowed him time to get far enough away, I took half the platoon after him. The wagon tracks were easy enough to follow. When I came to the tracks of the second set of wagons, I was damn well convinced your story had been right. The rest you know about.''

''I do indeed,'' Canyon said.

''I wouldn't have attacked with such force if I'd known you were inside,'' the major said.

''You did right. You did what you had to do,'' Canyon said.

''We're not entirely stupid, Agent O'Grady. We can be fooled, but we can recover. Put that in your report to Washington,'' Major Fisher said.

''Be glad to.'' Canyon smiled.

''We'll be taking all this silver back and exchange it for those stones we've been storing,'' Fisher said. ''We're much obliged to you, Agent O'Grady.''

''Any job that ends well is a good one,'' Canyon said. ''Now, has anyone seen a Colt with ivory grips? I wouldn't want to be losing that gun.''

''We have it here,'' the major said, and one of the soldiers brought the Colt over.

Canyon nodded in satisfaction as he stuffed it into its holster, walked to the palomino, and brought Blueberry's horse to her. He swung into the saddle and Blueberry followed as he walked the horse away from the cave.

''You've earned a rest, O'Grady. Relax and have a good trip back,'' Major Fisher called after him.

It was Blueberry who turned in the saddle, a smug little smile on her lips. "He will," she answered, and brought her horse alongside Canyon's as he started down the hillside passage.

"He will," Canyon echoed, turning the words in his mind. "I like a lass who can say a lot with a few words."

"Me too," she murmured.

KEEP A LOOKOUT!

**The following is the opening section from the
next novel in the action-packed new
Signet Western series
CANYON O'GRADY**

**CANYON O'GRADY #3
MACHINE GUN MADNESS**

*Short Creek, Missouri, eighty miles south of
Kansas City near the Kansas border, on July 14, 1860.
The trek to find Hirum Merchant and
his amazing new gun that fired
six hundred rounds a minute . . .*

Ten Osage warriors had been circling the small frame
house and yi-yipping just out of pistol range for a
half-hour. All of the warriors were mounted on war
ponies, all had bows and arrows, and one carried an
old flintlock rifle he might not know how to fire. They
darted in toward the door yelling and screaming, then
slanted away, guiding their horses with only their
knees.

Now one raced forward on his war pony and sent
an arrow smashing through the kitchen window.

Soon all of them shot arrows into the windows of
the small house. One of the braves paused at the side
to blow a coal into a flame, then he lit a torch and
raced toward the house.

Jolting through the yells and calls of the Osage came the snarling report of a heavy rifle. The warrior with the burning torch and a row of eagle feathers on his browband slammed off his war pony, a chunk of lead through his heart and lodged near his backbone. He sprawled in the Missouri dust never to move again.

Before the Indians realized they were under attack, a second report sounded and another Osage took a bullet high in the shoulder, sending him half off his pony. The warrior clung to the horse's mane, slumping forward as he raced off toward a creek a quarter of a mile away.

In a clump of brush two hundred yards from the house, a man lay, his eye pressed to the sight of a Spencer carbine. He tracked another Osage and fired. The attacking Indian took the round in his chest, screamed, and fell off his war pony.

Now the Indians looked in his direction, attracted by the pall of blue smoke the three shots had left just at the edge of the brush.

Four of the Osage turned and screeched at one another, then charged his position. The big man with a shock of flame-red hair who lay in the brush rolled toward a big cottonwood tree trunk and came to a kneeling position. He worked the trigger guard of the Spencer quickly, blasting lead at the charging Indians.

He knocked two of them off their horses before they were within fifty yards of him. They wheeled and headed back as he fired the last of the eight shots from the Spencer. He had drawn his big army percussion Colt revolver, but when he saw them wheel away, he upended the Spencer and quickly pulled out the empty tube from the butt of the weapon and pushed in a new tube filled with seven new rounds.

He chambered one and then sent six more shots at the Osage, who now streaked away, using the small house as cover against his rifle fire. When he was sure they were gone, the tall man rose and walked cautiously into the open, where he bent and checked the first of the fallen Indians. Two were dead. He had just bent over the third when a woman's voice cried out a warning.

He swung around, the Colt coming with him, and he fired automatically at one of the wounded Indians who had lifted up and started to throw a knife at him. The slug took the Osage in the left eye and drove him back into the dirt.

Canyon O'Grady checked the last two bodies, determined that they were dead, and looked up at the girl standing in the back door of the small house. First he saw the blue dress, nipped in at the waist and flaring at the breasts, buttoned protectively to wrist and chin.

Then he saw a billowing mass of long blond hair cascading around her shoulders and down her back. The six-gun she held seemed out of place, and he noted that wisps of gunsmoke still came from the muzzle. Her pale-green eyes looked up at him as he walked forward.

She saw a strapping man well over six feet, a shock of red hair and crackling blue eyes in a roguish face. She seemed to beat back tears as she smiled. "You saved my life. I thank you."

"Aye, lass. Osage, I'd say." There was a lilt of Ireland in his voice.

"Yes, they come through here now and then. Usually a shot or two near them and they move on."

"These were unusual, then."

She held the six-gun in front of her, not pointing it at him, but ready to. "You just passing by?"

"Might be. Looking for Hirum Merchant. In town they told me he lived here."

"Sometimes. He's gone right now. What would you want with him?"

"Business. Hear tell he's a gunsmith."

The girl nodded, her eyes a bit wary, blond hair rustling like ready-to-cut wheat. Now he saw that her nose was finely made, soft blond eyebrows, and a mouth that was set now in a firm pink line. A dimple would dent one cheek if she smiled, he was sure.

"Yes, Pa's an excellent gunsmith, but he doesn't hire out right now."

"Still and all, I need to see him."

"Likes of you is why he left two months ago. So many people came to see him he couldn't get his work done."

"That work he's doing is why I need to see him. I'd say I did you a favor, lass, with those Osage. Where I come from people are proud to repay favors. I think it's time for you to return the favor to me. The Osage were about to burn you right out of that house. I'd imagine you know what they'd do to the likes of a beautiful girl like you once you were out of rounds for that revolver of yours."

"I know what they would do." She sighed and lifted her glance to lock with his. The revolver swung down and she pointed it at the ground. "I'm truly grateful for your help. I was so frightened I could hardly shoot.

First I liked it out here away from the rest of town, but today I didn't.''

"I still need to find your father," he pressed.

He could see the emotions sweeping through her: gratitude to him, loyalty to her father. At last she sighed once more. "You come inside and I'll sit you down to some coffee and we'll talk some."

The house was neat, no dirty dishes on the ledge at the side of the kitchen. She took out a clean coffeepot and made a quick, fast-burning fire in a small cast-iron stove.

"Coffee be ready soon. I still can't tell you where Pa went. He made me promise. Said it was important that he get done with his work."

Canyon sat down in the offered chair and watched the sleek young woman getting the coffee started. When she turned, the movement brought the swell of her full breasts tight against the gingham dress. He watched in open admiration.

"The importance of your pa's work is why I'm here, Miss Merchant. My name is Canyon O'Grady, and I want to help your father get his work done."

"If you're looking to buy it, he isn't ready to sell."

"I don't want to buy it, lass."

"At least I know you're full of Irish blarney. I'm sorry, I can't help you."

Canyon looked out the window. "Time was when a person would be grateful for even the smallest favor. Now someone gets her life saved and it's good for only a fine thank-you and a beautiful smile."

"Pa said he was working on something important."

"That he is. The United States Army and the President of the United States are both highly interested in

Hirum Merchant's new rapid-firing gun. We know a little about it. We have also heard that others are trying to steal it from him.''

"The President of the United States?'' She looked up at him with awe, then suspicion. "The president? I really don't know whether to believe that or not.''

"You should. You probably haven't heard that there are a lot of people right now interested in making a gun like your father is working on. There are men from our own country who have said that they will find your father, steal his gun, and perhaps take him with them and set up shop to finish the gun and then begin to manufacture them. These men are well known for their crooked dealings and will stop at nothing to get what they want. The president sent me to find your father and protect him.''

The girl sat down slowly. "You really mean it, don't you?'' Her eyes went wide and she held out her hand. "Pleased to meet you, Canyon O'Grady. I'm Elizabeth Merchant.'' She continued to stare at him. "You actually talked to President Buchanan?''

"Yes, six or seven times. I work for him. That's why I'm here. We think your father needs some protection. We have information that at least one foreign nation, as well as this band of Americans, is out to get your father's invention away from him by any means possible.''

"Oh, they can't do that. Pa has worked on this new gun for over two years now. We've almost starved at times. Then he'd have to take work as a gunsmith at some town. But every night—'' Elizabeth stopped. "Oh, dear. I wonder if he's safe where he went? He didn't know somebody might actually try to steal the gun.''

''Someone could do far worse than that to your father, Miss Merchant.''

The pretty young woman frowned for a moment, then stood and paced up and down in the small kitchen. She looked at Canyon two or three times and finally stopped. ''Say Pa is in danger and there are these men trying to find and hurt him . . . How do I know that you're not just another one of them?''

''You have only my word on that, Miss Merchant. And my open, honest Irish face.''

''You don't have any kind of badge or a paper, or anything? Even a U.S. marshal has papers.''

He took a folded paper from his wallet. It was signed by President Buchanan and said Canyon O'Grady was a United States agent. Everyone was urged to give him complete cooperation.

She read the paper and gave it back to him, then went to the cupboard and took out a dish of ham and beans and put it in a pot she placed on the iron stove. Then she added two sticks to the fire. She poured the coffee and watched Canyon.

''I'm not sure I trust you, Canyon O'Grady. Irishmen are not my favorite people.''

Canyon grinned broadly. ''You're sounding a little Irish yourself. Samuel Johnson said, 'The Irish are a fair people, they never speak well of one another.' But then you know that Sam Johnson was an Englishman, so what can you expect?''

''Not saying I will, but if I was to be convinced I should take you to my pa, would you let me keep my six-gun?''

''Yes, I would. Two of them and a derringer and a knife if you want to carry them. But you don't have to take me anywhere. You can stay right here. Just tell me where he went so I can get to him as quickly as possible.''

"No, I won't tell you a thing. If I decide to, I'll take you there and watch you closely. There's too much blarney in you for my way of thinking.'' She stared at him a minute, then shrugged. "Near sundown now. If you split me some wood, I can finish warming us some supper. Tomorrow morning I'll decide what I'm going to do.''

"Where's the woodpile?''

A half-hour later Canyon came in with an armload of wood and stacked it neatly in the wood box. The supper was simple but adequate and the coffee hot.

When the dishes were put away, she pointed at the door. "Canyon O'Grady, take your Irish wit and your bedroll and find a spot to sleep in the woods. I'll be inside with the door bolted and broken windows covered—and my six-gun under my pillow. I'll decide to-morrow.''

"All right,'' Canyon agreed. "But I'll be ready to go tomorrow. I know you'll want the two of us to find your pa and warn him about the danger he's in.''

He watched her a moment and saw her working on the big problem. Then he said good night, went out the door, and waited until he heard the bolt slam home. Canyon found a spot in the brush where he had fired at the Indians. He wanted to give the redskins plenty of room to return and pick up their dead as soon as it was dark. He was surprised they hadn't done so already. They would float in during darkness like ghost dancers retrieving their slain friends and would be no threat. The Osage, like most Indians, do not like to fight at night.

Canyon stretched out on his bedroll. The girl was

worried about her father. He figured that she would decide, come morning, to go find him and would take Canyon along. There was really no other decision she could make.

Before he fell to sleep, Canyon went over his assignment again as he had been briefed by Major General Silas Warrenton. Many times President Buchanan himself gave Canyon his orders, but this problem was too urgent and there was no time for Canyon to go to Washington.

Canyon had been in St. Louis finishing up a case and had kept General Warrenton informed. He received a telegram a few days ago telling him to remain in place, a courier would be coming to hand-deliver a first-class secret document.

The courier met Canyon at his hotel, the Mid Western, had him write his name on a card, and compared it with a sample he brought with him. Then the courier took out a photograph and studied it against the real thing. When he was convinced that Canyon was who he said he was, he had him sign a receipt for the goods and went down to catch the next train back to Washington.

Canyon went up to his third-floor room and unsealed the envelope and began to read.

To: Canyon O'Grady, United States Agent.
From: Silas Warrenton, Major General USA., Military Aide to President Buchanan.

At once proceed to Kansas City, Missouri, and then south to a small town called Short Creek, and contact a gunsmith named Hirum Merchant.

Our information is that he is in the final stages of development of a new kind of rapid-firing gun that, if successful, will be a major leap forward in weaponry.

The United States government is interested in protecting Mr. Merchant from any outside influence, and wants to be sure that he has both the time and facilities to finish work on his weapon.

When you contact Mr. Merchant, explain to him the president's concern and urge him to be the guest of the government at the nearest United States military post or fort where he will be given space and equipment and board and room as he works on his project.

Problem: We are not sure that Mr. Merchant is at the above given town. He may have left. He has a daughter who may or may not be with him. Your first job is to find the man. Your second task is to protect him from all those who would try to buy, steal, or destroy his new weapon, and to safeguard Merchant himself.

Second problem is that there is at least one foreign power now in Missouri with several agents, determined to capture Mr. Merchant and steal his ideas, his prototype and plans, and perhaps kidnap Mr. Merchant himself and take him out of the country.

While preparing this briefing, I discover that there is now a second foreign power with several men in Missouri with the sole purpose of finding Mr. Merchant and evaluating his weapon. If they like it, they will attempt to buy it. If he won't sell, then they will simply steal it, probably kill Hirum Merchant, and return with the gun to their own nation. You must prevent this at all costs.

With the growing concern for finding new military weapons, our president feels that we must meet both of these threats by protecting Mr. Merchant.

You may requisition troops and weapons from any fort or army installation, including Fort Leavenworth just outside of Kansas City, Kansas. I have this day sent the fort commander a telegram authorizing such assistance from Fort Leavenworth.

Wire your receipt of these orders at once and wire me at any time you have need of assistance or direction and upon completion of the assignment.

There was the scrawled signature of General Warrenton at the bottom of the third sheet.

Canyon had sent a quick wire to Washington, put his magnificent palomino mount in a livery stable, and caught a night train to Kansas City. There was no way he could send his mount by train to Kansas City on such short notice. He bought a horse for the two-day ride to Short Creek, which had no stage service.

Now laying in the brush up from the house, Canyon heard something. He looked back at the house. A figure ran silently toward the building, then went around it and soon found one of the Indian bodies. The warrior picked up the corpse, looked around, and then hurried into the darkness.

Canyon saw two other Osage retrieving their dead, then the stillness was complete again. He waited for a half-hour, and when the Indians didn't return, closed his eyes and went to sleep. If anything moved within fifty feet of him, he would be awake instantly with his big army revolver in his fist.

Morning came suddenly on the plains with the sun bursting over the flatland horizon a hundred miles away, or so it seemed. Canyon was up and had slipped into his boots and gun belt, then shaved with cold water from his canteen. He sliced the whiskers off with a straight razor by feel. One of these days he was going to get a small metal mirror to carry with him.

He heard the house door open. Elizabeth came out, looked around, and went to the outhouse. She carried the revolver. He thought it was big enough to make a nasty hole. Canyon packed up his gear and tied it on his saddle, tightened up the cinch, and led the big bay mare down to the edge of the creek, where she drank her fill. He ground-tied her in some fresh grass and walked back to the house.

Elizabeth had just arrived at the door when he got there.

" 'Morning," he said.

She stared up at him and she looked as if she hadn't slept too well. "All right, all right, I've decided to lead you to where my pa is supposed to be. If all this is true you've been telling me, he might have left that spot as well, but we'll go and try to find him."

"Good, I was hoping you would say that."

"I've traveled before. I have a sack of food ready. Some bacon, eggs in a jar, two loaves of bread I baked yesterday, and some tins and dried goods. Couple of pots and a frying pan. You might find us a rabbit along the way. Breakfast first, flapjacks while we still have milk and syrup."

They left a half-hour later. She closed the door,

locked it, and put the key on top the door frame. Then she turned and frowned at him, her pretty face tense. "Just so we get this straight. You are coming with me, not the other way around. I know where we're going. I also have my thirty-two-caliber six-gun and I know how to use it. Right now I don't have any good reason to distrust you, and I hope it stays that way." She watched him a moment. "Any comments?"

"Only that you don't have to frown so much. It ruins your beautiful smile."

"Blarney will get you nowhere with me, Mr. O'Grady. Now let's ride."

They turned south and a little west. Canyon had admired the sleek way she fit into the ladies' riding trousers that she had on. They outlined her round little bottom delightfully. She wore a brown blouse and a light jacket and a straw hat with a wide brim with a tie under her chin.

She set a good pace down a country road, across a field, and toward the early-morning smokes of a village five miles away. They had just passed through a grove of trees when Canyon called sharply.

"Elizabeth, we've got company. Back to those trees, right now."

She saw the five men racing toward them across the field from the direction they had come. They were still three hundred yards away but coming at a gallop.

Canyon checked to see that the new Spencer carbine was still in his saddle boot, then kicked the bay in the flanks and surged into the brushline. He tied his mount, grabbed the Spencer, and ran to the edge of the brush.

Only two of them came straight on. The other three had circled around to the side.

"Damn," Canyon spat. Whoever it was planned on making a fight of it. So be it, Canyon growled to himself. He lifted the Spencer and sent a round over the heads of the two onrushing men, who were waving revolvers in the air. He'd find out quickly how serious they were about a fight.

There's an epidemic with 27 million victims. And no visible symptoms.

It's an epidemic of people who can't read.

Believe it or not, 27 million Americans are functionally illiterate, about one adult in five.

The solution to this problem is you... when you join the fight against illiteracy. So call the Coalition for Literacy at toll-free **1-800-228-8813** and volunteer.

Volunteer Against Illiteracy. The only degree you need is a degree of caring.